THE FURY OF KANTA

THE WOLVES OF KANTA
BOOK 4

MARLENA FRANK

Edited by: Lara Zielinksy
http://lzedits.com

Cover Art by: Harvest Moon Designs
https://www.facebook.com/groups/HarvestMoonDesigns

Map by: Kelley M. Frank
http://morbidsmile.com

Note: This is a work of fiction. Names, Characters, Places, and Events
are products of the author's imagination, and are used factitiously.
These are not to be construed or associated otherwise. Any resemblance
to actual locations, incidents, organizations, or people (living or
deceased) is entirely coincidental.

EB ISBN: 978-1-955854-12-2
PB ISBN: 978-1-955854-13-9
HB ISBN: 978-1-955854-14-6

To Aryn and Kyle
For supporting me, believing in me,
and inspiring me.

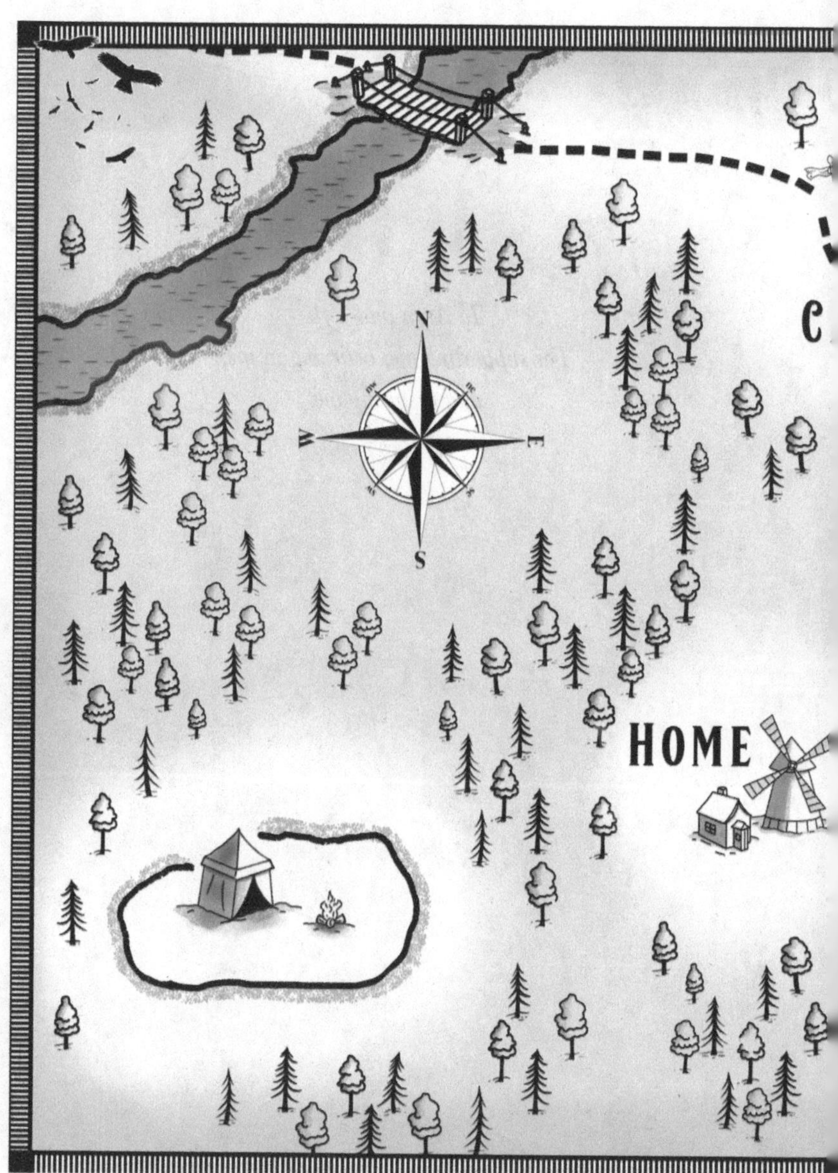

N
W
E
S
HOME
C

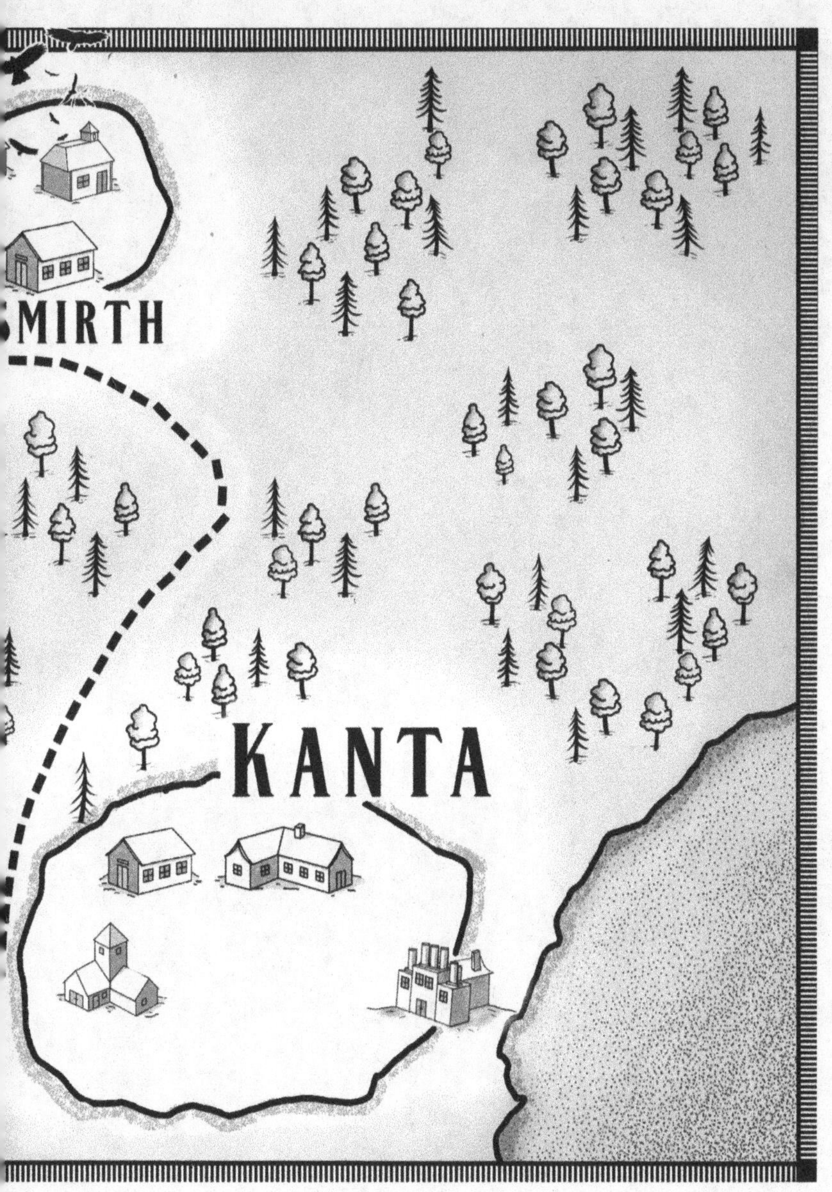

MIRTH
KANTA

PART 1

FAMILIAR PLACES

GOOD GIRL

FATHER WAS COOKING on the stove and filling the air with the scent of venison. Her mouth watered. He hadn't hunted for food for them in a long time.

Mercy must have fallen asleep on the couch. A pit of worry filled her stomach. He hated when she fell asleep anywhere but on the bed. She quickly wiped the drool from her lips and sat up straight on the couch. Father flipped the piece of meat on the frying pan with an explosion of hisses and sputters. Her stomach growled in response.

"Did you sleep well?" he asked, his voice calm and collected. It made Mercy panic. He was never calm and collected, especially not around her. She was always in trouble for some mistake or another, even if she didn't know what she had done wrong.

Father glanced toward her. The fire from the fireplace cast wild shadows across his face, making it hard to read his expression. Shadows flicked across the wooden floorboards of their kitchen like tendrils reaching out for her. It was unsettling.

"Come over here," he said.

Without question, Mercy got to her feet. It was a hard-wired response. She always did whatever her father asked of her, obedient to a fault. She came to his side and felt the fire hot against her face. Smoke from the meat made her eyes water and her stomach growled again. Her father didn't look at the venison spitting in the pan. He watched her instead. His cold, blue eyes pierced into her. Suddenly she worried she had forgotten something or missed some important task he had given her. Or maybe he was just annoyed she fell asleep on the couch. It wasn't always easy to figure out why he was mad, especially when it came to something she had done wrong.

"I'm sorry," she whispered, feeling like she was eight years old again and trying her best to impress him. She was always trying to make him happy even though she knew deep down that wasn't possible.

Father crouched down in front of her, sliding the knees of his worn jeans across the stone hearth. The firelight illuminated half of his face in brilliant gold and amber hues while the other half hid in shadow. He placed his hands on her shoulders, but his skin felt icy despite working over an open fire. That didn't make any sense, a part of her noted, but she pushed that thought away. Her father was back at her side again. Hot tears spilled from Mercy's eyes even though she didn't know why. What was there to cry over? She glanced around the room, but everything was in order. So why did she hurt so badly inside?

"Life's going to get a lot harder for you from here on out," he said. His voice kept cracking as though he was trying not to cry. "You've got to be brave, sweetheart. Can you do that for your dad, even though I was terrible to you?"

She nodded with enthusiasm. "I can be brave. I'm always brave." She smiled.

He clutched her shoulders tighter, his eyes bloodshot. "Promise me, Mercy. Promise your broken father you won't give up, no matter what happens. You might be too scared to go on, but you have to." Tears streamed down his cheeks into his stubble. She never saw him cry. He hated showing weakness in front of anyone but especially her.

She had seen him cry once, hadn't she? That terrible day with the truck and the traffickers and the werewolf cage. The last time she had seen him alive. A shiver went through her. His hand was bleeding. Mitchell and Carter had shot his hand. Then they shot him.

"I don't want to lose you again, Dad," she whispered.

He pulled her into a hug, wrapping his arms tight around her. She clung to him, crying harder. His arms were freezing, but she didn't care.

She knew he was dead. It didn't matter.

"I love you, sweetheart. I'm so sorry for everything." His stubble scraped at her cheek, against her ear. He felt so alive.

But he wasn't.

"I love you too, Dad." His shirt muffled her voice, so she tried again. "I love you too."

MERCY OPENED her eyes through tears that dripped down her cheeks.

"I love you too," she whispered, barely loud enough to hear. At first she thought she had fallen asleep on the couch again. No, she was inside of a cage. She reached a hand out, hoping she was still dreaming, but the iron bar was cold to the touch. She dragged her fingers down the rough metal and tears threatened to fall again. This was no dream.

The heat of the fire she had felt while asleep faded. Instead, a coldness chilled her. Slowly the sadness she felt morphed into outrage.

She knew this room. She had walked across it more times than she could count. She had learned how to walk against that wall holding her father's gentle hand. She recalled the feel of the wood against her bare feet. She knew its creaks and its groans, and where not to step because it would pinch her. It wasn't just the floors. Even the furniture was the same. The worn armchair and the rickety dining table with two chairs that never sat flat on the ground. The enormous fireplace and the woodpile nearby.

This was the living room she had grown up in. The house she had once called home.

It hadn't changed much since Mercy had been here last—early in the morning that terrible day when she ran inside briefly on her way to get electric prongs. The windmill had gotten stuck and she had to fix it too. Always in a hurry to get back to her disapproving father. A pain filled her chest and she closed her eyes against the memory, but it returned nonetheless. He stood outside the gate, chastising her without a word. She swallowed down the tears and opened her eyes again, trying to take in the home that still looked the same.

She hadn't meant to stay away forever. She always wanted to come back, but she never felt ready. It was too hard to face the mixed emotions she had of this house. In all honesty, she hadn't been sure if she ever would get the courage to come back. The thought of her past home crumbling and rotting away, being reclaimed by the wilderness, seemed fitting in a strange way. It had brought her comfort. Now, she saw her assumptions were wrong. Her home hadn't rotted away. Oscar had reclaimed it, kept it going. She should have expected it in a city full of opportunists like Kanta but still, it felt like an affront.

Now, here she was back home whether she wanted to be or not—in a werewolf cage like a wild animal.

Mercy got to her feet, moving slowly because her head felt heavy. She vaguely remembered Oscar dosing her with some kind of powder, but her final minutes in Crowsmirth were foggy and uncertain. Had Andrei and Kit left her behind on purpose? Had they glanced back but kept going? Or was her own imagination filling in the blanks? She shook herself, daring not to go down that dark path. Instead she focused on where she was.

The living room was in the same setup that she left it

that day. The armchair was in the same place, and their tiny dining set near the hearth right where they had left them. She half expected her father to walk through the front door and yell at her for playing in a werewolf cage. The thought made her head pound.

Perhaps Oscar was taking advantage of a free home with built-in protection. If that was the case, why did he go to Crowsmirth and risk being killed by werewolves? It didn't make any sense.

The floor was cleaner than she and her father ever used to keep it, and the fireplace had been swept recently. The small kitchen was clean, with no dirty dishes on the counters, and the dining chairs were all pushed in.

Whoever Oscar was, he certainly was a stickler for cleanliness. For some reason that made her more worried. What was he hiding? If he had wanted this home for himself, why leave it like a perfectly preserved specimen of its former self? It made her skin crawl. She trusted her instincts and right now they were screaming at her to get out.

With one hand on her throbbing temple, she took a close look at the door to the werewolf cage. She had worked with cages like that all her life and knew the various locking mechanisms well. She pushed her hands through the gaps between the bars and fiddled with the lock. The cage itself was old, but the lock was a newer model. A shiny new lock pin had been dropped into place to keep the door closed. Not a problem. She had worked with all the different models inside of Farrell Mill. Doing it backwards was a different matter.

She angled the metal lock pin, and moved it sideways as needed before straightening it out again. She did it wrong twice, but calmly she corrected herself. She would have to thank Thomas for showing her how to work with all the locks. She knew some from working under her father, but Thomas worked with all of them.

"There!" she whispered as she freed the lock pin from the door. It landed in her fingers, slipped through them, and fell to the ground, hitting the edge of the cage. A metallic gong reverberated throughout the room. Mercy winced. Doing it backwards was harder than she thought. She looked to the hallway toward the bedrooms, then she glanced to the front door and then the back door. No movement. With a shaky breath, she pushed the door open. It squealed on unoiled hinges and Mercy's heart leaped into her throat. She swallowed down the nerves, and then moved with smooth, deliberate motions. One leg, then two legs out of the cage, and then she carefully tipped the cage door against the wall.

Her heart thundered in her chest. She was free, at least partially.

She still wore her same clothes from Crowsmirth, except for the satchel of needles and the holster for her gun. That didn't matter. All she had to do was reach the woods and she was home free. She wouldn't even have to worry about werewolves since it was daytime.

She headed for the front door with quiet footsteps. Her father would be so proud. A noise off to the side sent a jolt through her. She pulled back from the door and glanced down the hallway toward the bedrooms. A woman with golden brown skin and her hair up in a wrap on top of her head moved from Mercy's bedroom to her father's room. She was humming to herself.

Mercy blinked.

Who was she? Was she cleaning the house? Did Oscar have a wife or a daughter she didn't know about? Or was she trapped in this place the same as Mercy?

She thought about going to help her, but then she thought better of it. The woman could be on Oscar's side. She could be working with him. No, she had to focus on herself first. Mercy could always return with Thomas, Andrei, and Kit. They could bring weapons if needed. She needed to get free first. Then she could try to help out others under Oscar's thumb.

Mercy waited until the woman moved farther into the bedroom, then she went for the door. She expected to need to unlock the handle or unlatch the deadbolt, but it turned easily in her hand and opened with a creak.

She froze. It would have made more sense to have to fight to escape. Oscar could have put a padlock on the cage or even one on the front door. This was too easy. It felt as if he wanted her to escape. Why go through all the trouble of kidnapping her only to let her leave so easily? None of this made any sense and the further she got, the more uneasy she felt.

With her heart pounding in her chest and her head throbbing, Mercy opened the front door, stepped out onto the porch, and quietly closed it behind her.

She breathed in the fresh air and for a moment felt like she had finally made it, finally found freedom.

Until she heard a growl beside her.

Mercy turned. A large silver werewolf stood just a few feet away from the porch. Around its neck she spotted a heavy metallic collar, not unlike the ones they used at the mill. It was attached to a chain. Several coils showed it wasn't a short chain. Mercy glanced to the front door and then back to the werewolf, before she looked to the gate on the electrified fence not far beyond.

She had run that distance many times in her youth and never thought much of it. Now she wasn't sure she could make it, but she had to try. She refused to return to that cage, so the only option was to run for it.

Trying to outrun a werewolf was a foolish move. She knew that. She had seen firsthand how fast they were, but she had to give it a shot. Despite her years of handling werewolves, she was quickly learning Oscar was a completely different beast.

Mercy leaped off the porch, hitting the grass hard, and took off at a sprint. She pumped her legs despite the throb in her skull. She kept her eyes on the gate. She had to make it. There was no other choice.

Behind her came the heavy footfalls of the werewolf. Then it howled. The sheer volume put ice into her veins. Mercy whimpered as she ran. From the corner of her eye she spotted a man sitting on the ground, pale and watching in shock under a brightly colored patch quilt. She looked twice, taken by surprise. He too had a heavy collar around his neck and a chain along with it. What in the world was going on here?

Hot breath drifted against the hairs on the back of

her neck and she pumped her legs harder even though her muscles burned.

Almost there, she thought to herself. *Keep going!*

The werewolf snarled as it ran, gaining ground fast. Its teeth clomped down behind her with a snap. She shrieked. The gate was still so far away. No way she could make it on foot.

This was why Oscar didn't care if she left. She couldn't get far. Nobody could.

Mercy didn't dare blink or slow down. Not when it tried to take another bite and some of her shirt got ripped along the back. No blood drawn—not yet at least. Tears sprung to her eyes and her throat burned.

The panting suddenly stopped with a grunt. Mercy knew what that meant. She had studied their hunting tactics for years with her father.

It had gotten tired of trying to bite at her. Instead, it leaped into the air. It likely was going to slam into her any second and crush her bones in the impact.

Mercy dropped to the ground so fast she almost tumbled forward, then she rolled her body to the side. The beast landed inches away from her, tossing dirt into the air. She clenched her teeth and scrambled for her life away from it. She caught sight of its eyes briefly and saw they were blood red. The eyes of the hunt and hunger.

She saw stars in her vision from pushing herself too hard and she struggled to get her body to move fast enough again. The werewolf stalked toward her, taking its time, knowing she had nowhere to run. Mercy gulped down air, breathing in the gritty dirt, and swallowed down the acrid taste of blood in the back of her throat.

"I'm sorry, Dad," she whispered and shook her head. She remembered her father's embrace in the dream and his words of caution. He had warned her how difficult it would be, hadn't he? She had thought she knew better. She always thought she knew better.

The werewolf opened its jaw, dripping saliva down onto the sparse grass. Its breath smelled like a carcass. Mercy wanted to close her eyes, but she didn't. She wanted to keep her eyes open and be aware. She had lived most of her life with her eyes closed to the truth of the world. She refused to die the same way.

A gunshot rang out. Mercy jumped. The pale man on the ground screamed.

The werewolf swung its silver head to the side, looking back toward the house. His nostrils flared as the urge to kill gave way to fear. His red eyes shifted to amber as he glanced back down to Mercy.

"Don't make me have to fire twice now." Carrying a shotgun, Oscar closed the front door behind him. His voice was calm but miffed, as though scaring off a transformed werewolf was a trivial task. "Next time won't be a warning shot." His slow, plodding footsteps crunched in the grass.

Mercy winced at knowing Oscar had seen her, knew she had tried to escape, and saw just how far that had gotten her. She glanced toward the pale man on the ground. He looked terrified. Clutching the brightly colored quilt tight around him, he scooted away from Oscar, dragging his chain leash on the ground.

As Oscar got closer, the gray werewolf whimpered a few times before scampering off. If Oscar's presence was intimidating enough to scare off a fully transformed werewolf, that didn't bode well for her.

Oscar came over to stand before Mercy. He had changed out of the white linen clothes of an innkeeper and into the leathers and hides of a hunter. His heavy brown boots weren't laced, but they had been worn for so long they had conformed to his feet. His shotgun was worn with age and use. The butt looked like it had been damaged at some point. Half of it was made of a different kind of wood from a repair. His close-cut black hair accented the warmth of his brown eyes and tawny skin. He looked like a kind, older man with large, empathetic eyes, but Mercy knew that couldn't be farther from the truth. She had been fooled by his kindly appearance at Crowsmirth. Now she knew it was merely a facade.

"You ought to be more careful roaming around on your own, Mercy. That was real close there. You could have been killed." Despite the concern of his words, a cruel smile curved his lips. It made her skin crawl. "Do you need help finding your feet?" he asked, but he held no hand out for her. In fact, all he did was cradle that shotgun.

Mercy was tired of playing his games. She was tired of being the butt of his joke and mocked at every turn. "Why did you bring me here? What do you want of me?"

His disturbing smile shifted into a horrid grimace that lit his eyes with anger. Mercy swallowed down her fear.

"It's improper for a young lady to talk to me like that while sitting on the ground. Get on your feet, girl."

Balling her hands into fists in the dirt, she spat. "No."

Oscar snorted, then calmly he placed the muzzle beneath Mercy's chin right in front of her throat. She broke out in a cold sweat. Maybe she should have followed his orders.

"With an attitude like that, I might have to train you like I do the wolves." He shook his head in disappointment. "I don't want to have to do that to you. If I wanted you dead, I would have shot you at Crowsmirth. But I don't have patience for a troublemaker either."

He pressed the muzzle against the soft skin of her throat. It was still hot from the gunshot earlier and she involuntarily whimpered.

"Now, stand up. I won't ask you again."

Taking a shaky breath, Mercy slowly crawled to her feet, pulling her throat away from the barrel and taking a step back away from him.

"There's a good girl. I'm glad to see Solomon taught you to respect your elders at least. Now get over here and make yourself useful. If you try for that gate again, mark my words. You won't make it. I guarantee I can shoot faster than you can run, child. You understand?"

Mercy nodded. "I understand."

OSCAR LED Mercy to where the pale man with the collar and chain sat on the ground. As they approached, he gripped the colored quilt tighter around him and looked nervously between them. His pale face was sunburned along with his left arm. He had clearly been out here a while.

Mercy thought back to when Oscar kidnapped her. She remembered hearing someone in the truck bed while she was put into the seat beside Oscar. Was this man kidnapped at the same time she was?

"Hello there, friend," Oscar said in greeting. "What do you call yourself?" Despite his cheerful greeting, Mercy noted he still held his shotgun at the ready.

The pale man was shaking, clearly terrified. He had shoulder-length chestnut hair and bloodshot eyes filled with tears. "Jamison." His voice was hoarse, as if he had been chained out here for days without water or he had been screaming at the top of his lungs. Possibly both.

"Ah, Jamison, that's a good name." Oscar nodded. "Good to meet you. My name is Oscar, and this here is Mercy. Say hello, Mercy."

She glanced at Oscar, and he gave her that grimace again. "Hi," she said. She was terse because she didn't know where this was going, and the longer these introductions went on, the more uncomfortable she felt with all of this. She wasn't sure what was going to happen here, but knew it wasn't going to be good.

Never relaxing his grip on his shotgun, Oscar turned to the man again. "Now, son, I bet you're wondering where you are. I'm afraid it wouldn't do much good to tell you."

"In the middle of nowhere is where we are, I know that for certain." Jamison gave a nervous sound like a mix between a sob and a laugh. He dragged a hand over his face and wiped away tears. "I've been screaming for hours."

"Yeah I heard," Oscar said. "I trust you realize now that nobody is coming to help you. Sorry about that, friend. It's by design."

Oscar relaxed his gun and pulled out a dart from his pocket. Mercy's eyes went wide. She recognized that dart. She had made dozens of them for her father. It even had the same feathers along the base. Oscar must have found the stash they kept, all prepared with Liquid Lead. She balled her hands into fists.

"So, Jamison," Oscar said with a smile on his lips. "Do you know what Liquid Lead is?"

Jamison nodded as his brows scrunched up with worry. "Why does it have to be Liquid Lead? I haven't done anything to you!" He wiped at his face again, his face getting redder. "Please, don't. I don't know who you are, but if I hurt someone close to you, if I broke a law or something, I promise I didn't mean to."

Oscar laughed, and a chill went down Mercy's spine. His sheer joy at tormenting this man was disgusting.

"You're a werewolf. You've probably eaten dozens of people. But I frankly don't give a damn about them. Not a single one."

"But why?" Jamison asked.

"You drew a bad hand is all. Went to the wrong part of town on the wrong day and met me." Oscar grinned. "You're the unlucky winner of the worst lottery, friend. You got caught by me last night, and now you get to be my guard werewolf for the rest of your days. Does that sound fun to you?"

Jamison started crying. "Please no! I didn't do anything to you!"

Oscar chuckled. "No, not to me. But you're a werewolf, so you're not really human, are you, friend?"

"I'm sorry! I never wanted to be a werewolf. I survived a bite months ago. I didn't want to be turned into this!"

"I'm sure you didn't." Oscar held up the dart. "Do you know what Liquid Lead does?"

Jamison barked a nervous cry. "No, I don't! If you're going to give it to me, just do it already! Why are you even telling me all of this?"

"No need to be hasty! I'm just explaining the facts is all. This here Liquid Lead is going to take away your mind and force you to live as a beast for the rest of your life. And as I said, you'll serve me until I'm through with you. Then I'll put you out of your misery. Now, how does that sound?"

The man gaped at him before deflating and curling inward on himself. It was as if he simply lost the will to fight. He looked up at the brilliant blue sky and autumn leaves. "Just get it over with, you monster."

Oscar pulled out one of the tubes Mercy had seen her father use many times. Those were things she couldn't make. They only had a few of them and she had maintained them, preventing them from getting any rust or damage. When he slid the dart into the tube, she shivered. Instead of administering it to Jamison, he turned to Mercy with an unsettling gleam in his eyes. "Here you go, Mercy. Take care of him, won't you?"

Mercy's jaw dropped. "What? You want me to do it?"

Jamison was sobbing, pressing his palms to his face, and rocking back and forth.

"Look at him. He's a broken man. Probably has been since he got that infectious bite." He smiled. "But the wolf in him won't be broken. He's got a bit of life left in him, and we can use that, you and I. Dose him with it."

She looked from the tube to Jamison and back up at Oscar. This monster didn't know the full depths of his actions, or how much this would hurt her to do. He didn't know all of her failed experiments with Liquid Lead. He didn't know Mercy had lost tentative friendships because of her inability to cure it. All he saw was an easy way to make a guard dog from a man.

"No, please. Don't make me do this," she whispered.

Oscar arched his eyebrows. "Make you do this? Isn't this what your old man taught you to do as a child? This really shouldn't bother you so much, child."

Mercy didn't respond. She wasn't sure what to even say.

Oscar leaned in closer. "Did you forget the threat I made just a minute ago?" He held up his shotgun in one hand. "You live by my rules here. This is no time to grow a spine, child. I don't want to shoot you, but I won't hesitate if you disobey me again. I said dose him and be quick about it. We don't have all day for this nonsense."

He shoved the tube with the dart into Mercy's hands. She stared down at it, regretting ever making the darts and for carelessly leaving them here for Oscar to find. Did she really think this place would simply rot and wouldn't be ransacked while she was away? How could she have been so foolish to assume this place would stay protected without her here?

Jamison held the blanket up over his mouth. He stared at Mercy with red eyes. "Please… don't do it. I promise I'll do anything you want, just don't dose me with that. I don't want to lose my mind."

Oscar held his shotgun again in both hands and took a step back. Mercy knew what that meant. With trembling fingers, she removed the dart from the tube and walked up to Jamison. She took a deep breath and stared into his tear-filled gaze.

"I'm sorry," she whispered. Then she jabbed the needle into his neck.

Jamison cried out and Mercy hurriedly stepped back, not at all sure what to expect. She had never seen Liquid Lead given to a werewolf when they weren't transformed. A part of her hoped Oscar was wrong and Jamison would stay human. Then Jamison's change started and she felt a part of herself break for him.

"There's a good girl," Oscar said, placing a hand on her shoulder just as he had done in Crowsmirth.

His touch made her lip curl. She shoved the hand off of her and stepped away from him.

"Not one for compliments, I see!" Oscar laughed.

Oscar headed back to the porch, urging Mercy to follow him. She did follow, but couldn't help watching

Jamison's full transformation. Soon he stood up as a tall, brown werewolf. She had seen Andrei transform many times, but it was more horrific to see it in the full light of day. As soon as Jamison spotted them, his eyes went red with rage and he raced toward them.

Mercy gasped and stepped farther up the porch on reflex. The slack on Jamison's chain seemed to go on forever as he got closer and closer.

"Oscar?" she asked, taking another step back.

"Now you're scared of him," Oscar said with a laugh. Mercy didn't see the joke.

Just before he reached the porch, Jamison hit the end of the slack and his collar choked him. He backed up a step, then two. He shook himself before going back to snarling and biting at them.

Oscar laughed. "I much prefer his wolf side, don't you?"

She shook her head, pursing her lips. "Why did you do that to him? Why did you kidnap him just to bring him here and tie him up? Surely, it's more than needing a guard werewolf when you already have one." She gestured to the silver one, still watching them from his post.

Oscar gave her a wide, toothy grin. "Well, that's simple. I need two to keep the gate protected. Don't want anything nasty getting inside, do we? Werewolves might be deterred by that fence but I bet a hunter or two could find a way past that gate. I bet you know how to get through it even with the windmill going, don't you?"

Mercy didn't respond.

"But even the most brazen hunter in Kanta wouldn't

dare get near a pair of fully transformed werewolves. One, maybe. But two? Not worth the trouble for most people. Besides, now I have one more guard to keep you from running away." He laughed. "So thank you for your help, Mercy."

She closed her eyes and reminded herself Oscar still held a shotgun in his hands. She took a deep breath to keep from saying something she might regret, but she wasn't sure how long she would be able to hold her tongue with Oscar constantly egging her to lose her temper.

"Now get inside. These beasts out here are dangerous. It's no place for a young lady."

Somehow Mercy didn't think inside was going to be much better.

2

PAINFUL LESSONS

MERCY COULDN'T HELP NOTICING the difference in behavior between the silver werewolf and Jamison. While Jamison was feral, trying to kill them almost as soon as he transformed, the silver one just sat and watched them from a distance. Mercy couldn't help but wonder how many times Oscar had shot the silver one to teach them not to approach when he held the shotgun. One time? Twenty? She wondered how many werewolves survived it and how many didn't.

Back when Mercy worked as an assistant at Farrell Mill, it was her job to take care of the female werewolves that had been given Liquid Lead. They weren't ferocious like Jamison had become upon being given a dose. They were humans trapped in beastly bodies, their minds intact even if they had no voice. Mercy worked for months feeding them, cleaning their cages, and even maintaining the grinders. It was only when Thomas trusted her to help with his research that she was able to dabble in the chemicals that led to her discovery.

Mercy created what she considered a partial cure. Given to a werewolf who hadn't been given Liquid Lead, it would allow them to transform themselves at will, no longer tethered to the night. Mercy took copious notes during her time as a researcher, and she understood the physiology of werewolves probably better than they did.

Werewolves healed quickly. She had seen that in her research, but some didn't heal as quickly as others. She suspected diet and age played a big part in that, but she hadn't wanted to conduct that level of research on her werewolves at Farrell Mill. She didn't want to hurt the people who were dependent on her for their safety. Oscar apparently didn't have her same concerns.

When she stepped through the front door, the woman from before stood in the hallway holding a basket of linen. Mercy saw her face and realized she knew her. It was Rose from the Kanta werewolf camp, Leyda's love who they all believed was dead.

"Is the second guard wolf prepared then?" Rose asked Oscar. She didn't even look at Mercy.

"All is well again," Oscar said. "And you didn't have to watch it this time. Aren't you glad?"

A shadow fell over Rose's face and she looked away, holding one hand balled against her chest.

"Rose?" Mercy asked.

Rose gave her a halfhearted smile, but she didn't say a word. Was she afraid to say anything? Or maybe she didn't recognize Mercy? It had been a long time ago, over a year. Maybe she simply didn't remember her.

"We didn't see you at the camp," Mercy blurted, so

glad to see someone she knew. The fact Rose didn't even acknowledge her was just too much after Jamison. She couldn't help more words tumbling out. "Everyone thought you were dead. Nobody had seen you in ages. And Leyda—"

Shoved forward between her shoulder blades, Mercy was cut off. She barely kept her balance as she stumbled forward. Rose quickly backed away, clutching her basket of linens and keeping one fist against her chest.

"Stop gawking and carrying on, girl! Rose has work to get done. Don't you, Rose?"

Rose nodded and went down the hallway, back toward the bedrooms. She didn't look back at Mercy and she didn't say another word.

Mercy gritted her teeth and climbed to her feet. Turning toward Oscar, she pushed through the pain of her throbbing back.

"Don't delay Rose. She has important work around here, and the less I see you two gossiping, the better." Oscar gestured to the living room and Mercy entered the room. She headed for the armchair near the fireplace.

"No, you don't get that seat."

Mercy froze and looked back at him. She didn't dare test him when he had that tone.

"Only well-behaved children get chairs. You nearly made me have to shoot you out there. You have to earn the ability to have a chair." He thumbed toward the cage. "Get in there. That'll be your home for a few days until you can decide to cooperate."

Mercy gaped at him. She did not dare openly

protest, but she was also horrified at being kept in a cage. She had taken care of so many werewolves in cages and knew exactly what that life was like. She wasn't sure if she would ever get out if she went into it again.

"You disappoint me, Mercy. I didn't expect you to be so rebellious, but I guess, considering your old man, I should have expected it." He sighed. "I really don't want to shoot you, but you sure are trying my patience. Get in the damn cage and quit making a scene."

Mercy bit her tongue to keep from voicing a retort and climbed back into her cage, even though every part of her body cried out against it.

He might never let her out again. He could shoot her in here. He could starve her or make her die of thirst. But, she reminded herself, he could do all of those things from outside the cage too. If she wanted to survive to get out of this horrible place, she had to do as he said. She had no choice. Either obey and play along with Oscar's cruel game or get shot and killed in her childhood home.

She crawled across the cold metal and sat with her back against the bars closest to the wall. Bringing up her knees, she wrapped her arms around them.

Oscar gave an approving nod. "And not a nasty word out of you. That's more like it. See, that wasn't so hard, was it?" He pulled a padlock out of his pocket and locked up the door. Mercy's stomach fluttered as the lock clinked closed. It took all of her willpower to keep from kicking the door open and making another run for it. Oscar studied her with a cold stare.

This had been a test, she realized, and she had failed it. That was why the door had been left unlocked. Oscar had waited to dose Jamison with Liquid Lead. All a test, and maybe a manipulation tactic too. She had gotten a taste of freedom and now it was taken away until she could prove she could follow orders.

Orders had always been difficult for her. Gripping her hands tight around her legs, she forced herself to be still, allowing herself to be locked up by the monster who now controlled her freedom.

He grabbed the padlock and gave it a good shake, watching her all the while for a reaction. Another test. Another attempt to ruffle her feathers and see a reaction. Mercy pressed her lips tightly closed. She wouldn't give him the satisfaction of watching her cry or scream. She wouldn't even struggle while he watched. He expected that. Possibly he had some malice that wanted to see her try.

Oscar chuckled and shook his head. "You're one tough cookie, aren't you, child?"

Mercy stared at him in silence.

He shrugged. "I like it. That's all I'm saying. I like seeing that fight in you. It's healthy." He pulled one of the dining chairs over to face her cage and sprawled down in it, propping the shotgun at his side. "Feeling quiet after that business with Rose, aren't you? That's alright. I'm sure I can talk enough for the both of us."

She took a deep breath and felt the pain throb between her shoulder blades. She had to play along. She had no other choice. Still she bristled. She had never handled authority well and Oscar seemed to enjoy playing with her rage. It was bad enough being his prisoner but hearing him talk down to her constantly was far too cruel.

Oscar leaned forward, and the chair creaked beneath him. He propped his elbows on his knees so that he was only a few feet away from the cage. "You have no idea who I am, do you?"

Mercy shook her head.

He pursed his lips. "Your old man never said a word about me all those years? Never mentioned old Oscar Krim?"

She knew she should hold her tongue, but Mercy had never been good at that and this man had the gall to bring up her dead father in the house he had built. He didn't deserve her patience. He deserved her fury. "My father didn't associate with low-life kidnappers, so no, he never mentioned you. Sorry for the disappointment."

Oscar chuckled and sat back in his chair. "There it is, the spitfire mouth I knew you had to have if you were Anna's daughter. You have her personality in so many ways." He pointed over his shoulder toward the fireplace. "I painted her. Did you know that? I painted that portrait of her and gave it to them on their wedding day. Solomon warmed up to it eventually, wanted to hang it in the main room. Anna was less thrilled with it but could never tell me why. She never could find a single flaw in it. Said it was perfect."

Mercy hated to admit it, but it was a beautiful painting. She had always thought so. Even though she hadn't gotten to meet her mother, she loved the expression of mirth on her mother's face; the smile was about to pull into a full laugh. It was horrible to think someone as sick as Oscar had painted it. It tarnished the joy in it somehow and made the painting take on a strange, creepy quality she hadn't noticed before. The colors were a little too bright and her mother's face a little too perfect. Or maybe she was just projecting Oscar's personality onto it.

No wonder her mom didn't like it but could never find a flaw. Mercy had to admit that even knowing its unhinged creator, she would have still put it up in a place of honor too. It had been a companion throughout her childhood, a glimpse into the life she could have had, and a perspective on her mother that she never would have had otherwise. She loved the comfort it gave her, especially when her father was in a foul mood. That painting was one of the few things she missed from her home.

"She and I knew each other for years," Oscar said, pulling Mercy's attention back to him as he puffed up with pride. "She and I were very close, Mercy, if you can believe that. If your foolish father hadn't stolen her heart away from me, I could have been your father. You could have been a Krim!" He laughed, "I bet you didn't expect that, did you?"

A pit formed in Mercy's stomach, but she pushed out a very polite, "No."

"Believe it or not, it's true!" He raked a hand through his brown hair and gave her a smile that still came across as cold with the loaded shotgun propped up at his side. "I often told her how I wanted children one day. She didn't seem very fond of the idea, or of me, to be honest. Every time I wanted to go out with her, she was always busy at the pub with her customers. Always putting other people before me." He shook his head. "Well, we can both see where that got her."

Mercy bristled. "My mother died in childbirth. It had nothing to do with her business. Besides, the werewolves started attacking every night. I'm pretty sure she had more important things to worry about besides your wounded pride."

"But that's just it." His smile fell away, and he gave her a cold, calculating stare. "If she had chosen me instead of your foolish father, she might still be alive."

That hit too hard. Mercy put a hand to her mouth and dropped her gaze. This man had a way of climbing under her skin that made her uncomfortable. His words were like dripping poison on her mind, until she couldn't take another word out of his mouth. She could face eccentrics like Thomas or vicious killers like Leyda, but Oscar was a different puzzle entirely. He reminded her of Carter or Mitchell, manipulating everyone around them to get what they wanted, whatever it took. The careless way he spoke about her parents, both of whom were now dead, made her insides quake with a mixture of hatred and anguish she had been trying very hard not to feel. Trust Oscar to find all the cracks in her carefully crafted armor.

Her gaze drew up to her mother's portrait, to the sparkle in her eyes and the wise retort on her lips. It pained her to know behind her mother's clear love of life she'd had to deal with Oscar, who likely had some cruelty to his nature even then. Had she been forced to deal with this man for years pining after her? She would never hear her mother's perspective on any of this, only Oscar's, and that seemed horribly unfair. She wondered if it had taken Mercy's callous and terse father to make her mom feel protected and loved.

At one point in her life, Mercy might have found the truth out from her father—assuming she could have eventually gotten him to give up his secrets. She suspected he never would have let Mercy know about Oscar, but he couldn't have known Oscar was still alive and still thinking about Anna so many years later. Now they were both dead, and Mercy had only Oscar's tainted words to pry the truth from.

"You loved them both, didn't you?" Oscar asked.

Mercy's eyes stung, and she didn't trust herself to speak and keep her voice steady, so she merely nodded.

"Anna… she meant the world to me. Some men say that about a woman and don't really mean it, but I do. I was devastated when she passed. But you… she gave her life to bring you into this world. You meant more to her than anyone, even Solomon."

Tears fell from Mercy's cheeks and she wiped them away, trying her best not to give Oscar the satisfaction of knowing he was getting to her. But Mercy had never spoken to anyone about her mother, and the pain of her father still felt too raw. She had thrown herself into her research to keep from facing it. Now the wounds were opening up fresh like he had died yesterday. Not that Oscar cared how much he hurt her.

He had been ready to shoot her in the throat mere minutes ago.

"Mercy, I can't bring back Solomon or Anna. I can't change what happened to them. But I knew deep down you hadn't met their same fate. They all said the werewolves got to you in the woods and dragged off your body, same as Solomon, but I knew better. I've seen the pieces the werewolves leave behind, the bloody husks just like I saw with your father's remains, and I knew—"

"Don't you ever stop?" Mercy cried, climbing to her feet. She was shaking from head to toe. "I don't know what you want from me or why you brought me here, but I can't listen to you talk about them like that!"

Oscar pursed his lips, seeming to size her up, but Mercy didn't care anymore. She would play his ridiculous games, stay in her cage like he asked, but she couldn't deal with him talking about her father's body like that. She hadn't even known the werewolves had left anything behind that night. The very thought of it made her stomach tighten and her vision go blurry. It was too new, too fresh, too painful.

"I know you don't like me. I know you want to escape and if you get the chance, I'm sure you'll make a run for it. You'll be running straight into a hunter's gun or a werewolf attack like you did at Crowsmirth." He shook his head, "That isn't what I want for you, Mercy. I have you here for your own good. I want to help you."

She bared her teeth, stalking across the cage so that she was almost touching the bars opposite him. "How the hell do you think you can help me? You tried to kill me and now you have me locked up in this cage."

"Because you're home," Oscar said with a devious smile. "I knew you were out there somewhere. Eventually I knew I would find you." His face went serious. "I can be a better father to you. Better than Solomon ever was. If you can learn to trust me, Mercy, I can be the father you could have had. No, the father you *should* have had from the start."

Mercy stared at him in utter horror.

"We can have a family together, Mercy. That wouldn't be so terrible, right? You can live here with Rose and me. All you have to do is trust me."

A fire filled her, and all care for pleasing her captor flew out the window. The words fell like poison from her lips. "You are nothing like my father. You've lost your mind if you think I will ever trust you."

"Don't be too hasty, girl." Oscar sneered. "Living in a cage has a way of changing people. Don't let that temper put you in a bad position. You may regret it."

"I don't care how long you keep me here. I will never trust you or see you as anything other than my kidnapper." She slammed a hand against the bars and the sound reverberated through the metal. "You are not my father."

Oscar shot to his feet so fast Mercy gasped. He shouldered his shotgun in such a quick, fluid motion that she took a step back.

"Then I guess you need to get comfortable in that cage, child. Cause you sure aren't getting out with that attitude."

He stormed back outside and slammed the front door behind him. Mercy was left standing in the werewolf cage wondering if she had made the right decision and knowing she couldn't take it back, even if she had signed her own death certificate.

"Jamison, get back!" Oscar cried outside. A shotgun blast reverberated, and a werewolf howled in pain. Mercy had wound Oscar up and he was taking out his frustration on Jamison.

She winced with regret.

———

MERCY PACED IN HER CAGE. There wasn't much room for it, but she couldn't sit still. She couldn't let herself succumb to the hopelessness threatening to overwhelm her. Instead, she turned fear into anger.

At first, she had been frustrated with herself for being so stupid to try to escape. No hunter would ever really give their prey the chance to leave. Despite the gnawing feeling she could have gotten free if she had been a little faster or a little smarter, Mercy knew that was what Oscar wanted her to think. It was meant to make her doubt herself. Instead of giving in to self-hatred, she looked at Oscar. If she really wanted to get out of here, she had to understand the complex monster who was her captor.

He was fast on the draw—faster, she had to admit, than her father. She could imagine her dad's outrage at her even mentioning it, but she had to be honest. However, she noticed Oscar favored his right leg and walked with a limp. Was that from a werewolf attack or something else? Regardless, it was a weakness, and one to be carefully noted. Other than his left leg, he seemed to be in excellent health, especially at his age, assuming he was around her father's age. His mind, however, was a different story. He was strangely obsessed with Mercy's mother. Had he pined for her, for a woman who would never love him back? It sure did seem like it, especially when she looked at the painting he made of her. Now he wanted to pretend to be Mercy's father, as if he could even try to be as protective and loving as her real father. He was gross even to attempt it.

A shuffling sound drew Mercy away from her thoughts and she turned to see Rose carrying a fresh basket of linen inside through the backdoor. That meant there had to be a space outside for her to hang up clothes to dry. Which meant there was space in the back-yard where the werewolves couldn't reach. Mercy stored that nugget of information aside for later.

"Rose?" Mercy hissed to her, but she didn't turn to even look at her. She was a werewolf, so Mercy knew she could hear her. Mercy tried again. "Rose!"

Rose turned wide and fearful eyes on her.

"Please talk to me. You're the only one here who can help me."

Rose glanced at the front door. Oscar had gone outside and shot Jamison, but Mercy hadn't seen him since. It was unnerving how he just roamed the grounds with a gun and shot at the transformed werewolves at whim. Judging by Rose's clear fear, his intimidation tactics clearly worked. She looked like he might barge in through either door at any second. Dressed in a simple linen gown dyed a pale pink with a matching wrap around her hair, Rose approached Mercy with careful steps.

"Keep your voice down," Rose whispered. "The walls are thin, though you probably already know that. You've lived here longer than I have." She glanced again at the doors. "Don't you know that madman is always listening?"

Mercy gave a slow nod, pursing her lips before asking in a hushed whisper. "How did he get you?"

She pursed her lips as though weighing the risks of talking to her. She was taking short breaths and her basket of clean laundry shook in her hands. What in the world had Oscar done to her to make her so terrified?

"Captured me when I was changed," she said, putting a fist to her chest as though trying to keep her heart from pounding through her ribcage. "I woke up in this hell. He used that same cage on me too." She shook her head and came forward to put a hand against the bars. "You know Silver outside? The big werewolf? He fought back once. Oscar took off one of his limbs. He grew it back eventually, but it took a long time."

Mercy's eyes went wide.

"Now he's as calm as a kitten around him. I even saw him nervous pee once when Oscar walked past him." She shook her head, her brows furrowed with worry. "Oscar is brutal. He isn't just talking big when he makes threats. He carries through on his horrible actions. Trust me. My advice to you is this: do whatever he wants. It's easier that way. Trust me."

Mercy nodded. She remembered Silver whimpering when Oscar had merely stepped outside. Jamison would probably be docile like that too soon enough once Oscar shot him enough times. She shivered. How horrible.

"Just don't try to be brave and do something stupid." Rose reached through the bars and took Mercy's hand. "He said he needed someone to care for his house, so I agreed. As long as I stay on top of my chores, it's not a problem. Just save yourself the pain and do it. I don't want to see you killed."

Mercy squeezed her hand. "Please, you have to help me get out of here. You're my only hope, Rose. He wants me to pretend he's my father." Simply saying the words made her disgusted.

"Rose?" Oscar's call from the front yard made them both jump. Mercy felt a tremor go through Rose. Her hand shook in Mercy's grip.

"Seems like that's a small price to pay for your freedom," Rose snapped. "If you're smart, you'll play along. If you aren't, well, I guess you won't be living long anyway."

Rose tried to pull her hand away, but Mercy held it tight.

"It's not that easy for me. I can't do this. I can't pretend." Mercy's voice wavered. "Please!"

Rose leveled her with a hard stare. "If you're not smart enough to try, then you might as well let those werewolves outside gobble you up 'cause I sure as hell can't help you."

She snatched her hand back with a stern expression as the front door creaked open.

"And cool that temper." Rose's voice had dropped to a whisper. "He's killed people for far less than that little outburst you had earlier." She shifted the basket to her hip. "I should know. I had to clean up the bodies after the messes he's left behind."

Mercy gaped as Rose turned quickly to the front door to close it behind Oscar as he came inside.

"Didn't you hear me out there, you damn wolf?"

"I'm sorry, sir, I had my hands full." The slight tremor to Rose's voice made a drop of sweat go down Mercy's spine.

"Too busy to answer me back?" Oscar asked in a clipped tone. "Your hands were too full for your tongue to waggle, is that it?"

Rose's eyes were wide, but she didn't answer him.

"Or were you too busy talking to Mercy here? Already trying to conspire against me, are you?" He pulled off his gun and hung it up on the wall. "I should have known Mercy would try. But Rose, I expect more of you."

With a small gasp, Rose shook her head, trembling from head to toe. "No, sir, we didn't speak at all." She stepped away from him, putting her back up against the wall, but Oscar turned and quickly closed the distance between them.

"Not a word? Not even a little whisper between old friends?" His voice dipped menacingly. "Do you swear by that, Rose?"

A tear slipped down Rose's cheek, breathing hard as she averted her gaze from Oscar's cruel glare. She gave a small whimper in response and nodded her head, but couldn't look at him. Or perhaps she dared not look at him.

"I trust you, Rose dear. You know I do. Of all the disgusting wolves on my land, you're the only one with any sense around here. In fact, you're one of only a few that I've let live in my house and sleep in a real bed. You should feel lucky!"

Rose shook her head and pursed her lips, looking close to tears.

"I could easily dose you with Liquid Lead and send you out with the others. Put you on one side of the house or the other. Maybe even shoot you dead and drop you out for the werewolves to feed on. But I haven't done that to you. Do you know why that is?"

He bore down on her and Rose looked like she wanted to melt into the wall if she could. She started crouching down toward the floor.

"No, sir," she squeaked out in a faint voice.

"Because, unlike most of your monstrous kind, you fear me. And a wolf should fear mankind. All wolves ought to fear us. Do you know why, Rose?"

"Because we are animals?" she asked.

Oscar became animated, shaking his head and drawing his arm back. He drew something long and shiny from his belt loop. It was a set of prongs. Mercy's eyes went wide. He wound it up with practiced speed, arcing a spark between the spokes. Rose covered her head with her arms.

"I'm sorry." Rose whimpered. "Please don't!"

"No, please!" Mercy cried.

Oscar ignored them both and shoved it into Rose's side. A spark briefly lit up the corner of the room and Rose fell hard to the ground. Mercy had seen the strength of those prongs knocking werewolves back in cages when they were fully transformed.

"No! That is not why," Oscar roared. "Werewolves are not animals. Animals deserve our respect, our appreciation. Werewolves are an abomination. They should not exist. They are a horrible mixture of humanity and beast and are not fit to walk alongside mankind. As an abomination yourself, you ought to know this, Rose."

He shouted at her as though this was common knowledge, as though this was all scientific fact and not the mad ramblings of a cruel, abusive monster. Rose crouched on the floor whimpering and clutching at her side, surely in too much pain to hear much of his madness let alone care.

Oscar took a step back and gestured for the door. "Go on then, and don't forget your damn laundry."

Rose clambered to her feet and scurried out the front door, dragging the basket out with her. She still clutched at her side, groaning with pain.

The silence after her departure was deafening. Oscar stood there, shoulders rising and falling with deep breaths, before he reattached the prongs to his belt loop. He cracked his neck and stood up straighter as he walked over to Mercy's cage. He sat down in the wooden chair with a huff and stretched his bad leg out in front of him.

"Rose is a good kid, just doesn't always know when to say no. Like when she gets the chance to talk to an old friend who might want out of a cage." He looked up at Mercy with a smirk on his lips. "You're a bad influence on her." He dragged a hand through his thin black hair.

"Don't be fooled though, Mercy. She is still a wolf. She is just as conniving as the rest of them. Just as bloodthirsty. When the moon rises tonight, you'll see what I mean. She grows fur and fangs just like all the others." He pulled a flask from his pocket and took a swig.

"You're a madman. You deserve to be locked up for what you're doing here. Torturing people. Kidnapping. It's terrible."

He barked a laugh. "Oh, is that so? And who do you think would come down here to lock me up for all those terrible things I'm doing? The good sheriff down in Kanta? No, wait, he died last year, didn't he? I guess the newly promoted deputy sheriff then. I'm sure he'll care about some abused werewolves. I'm sure he'll be real softhearted after what happened to his predecessor Jacob Pillsby. Oh, what about those hunters down at Crowsmirth? There are lots of them. They surely have the numbers to come down here and teach me a thing or two. I'm sure they'll put a barricade up around my house and tell me not to hurt werewolves anymore. How many heads do you think they collected from that last stakeout they made? A dozen? Maybe even fifty?" He gave a little laugh before taking another swig from his flask. "Nobody gives a damn about a few hurt werewolves, child. Least of all anyone in town. Hell, they would probably praise me for doing good down here for once. I'm making use of the disease. Isn't that what Thomas Farrell does? Puts those werewolves to work! He gets praise all the time. Why should I be any different?"

Mercy balled her fists, hating that he was right but

also wanting to prove that he was wrong. He wasn't devoid of blame. Surely someone would try to put him away for the horror that took place here, the deaths, the torture. She searched for something—anything—she could say to hurt him.

"Once they find out you kidnapped me, then you'll really be in trouble. That's not legal!" As soon as she saw that disgusting grin of his, she knew she was wrong.

"You keep repeating these fairy tales your old man spoon fed you, don't you? Surely you don't believe in all this nonsense. Everybody knows that Kanta, Crowsmirth... Nothing legal happens here, child. That's why all those nobles up north pay per head and don't come down here themselves to do the work. They don't hire anybody to clear out these woods directly because they know how dangerous this land is." He gestured around the room. "This house, your father's land, is just a short drive from Kanta. Why, kidnapping women there is practically a secondary hobby. Second only to trapping werewolves, of course. If they found out I kidnapped you, some other hunters would come down and try to steal you away from me. They wouldn't care about your well-being. Not in the least. Don't fool yourself, child. There's nobody coming to rescue you. No law, no offi-cers, and certainly no hunters. People like you and me, we're on our own. The sooner you learn that, the sooner you can do as you please in this world."

Mercy realized with a horrible, sinking terror that Oscar might be right. That this horrible person who kidnapped people from the streets of Crowsmirth might not be doing anything legally wrong. The realization was stunning. It was the exact opposite of what her father had always taught her, but then again, he also had never wanted her to go to Kanta. He had never wanted her out of his sight.

Much like Oscar now.

3

ANNA'S PORTRAIT

ROSE CAME BY a few times more, always without speaking. She hadn't said a word to Mercy after her last punishment. She barely made eye contact with her, but she did bring her a wooden cup of water and a couple of slices of bread. Briefly Mercy considered using the wooden plateware as weapons, but she had nowhere to hide them. The cage left her exposed to everyone moving in and out of the home. She had no privacy here.

Mercy ate, drank, and studied the patterns of her captor's home. Oscar spent most of his time outdoors, but he burst in regularly. Probably keeping an eye on her. And discouraging any further attempts she and Rose might make to communicate. Rose spent more time indoors but since her punishment, she no longer acted as if Mercy even existed unless she was bringing food or removing plates.

Despite Mercy's best attempts to study her new surroundings, she felt tired after eating and sleep pulled at her. She hadn't slept properly since the night in the closet with Andrei, and she didn't consider the drug that had knocked her out to be a proper sleep either. Her body was clearly still recovering. She leaned up against the bars, intending to close her eyes for a brief few minutes. Instead she was consumed by sleep entirely.

Her dreams reflected her waking terror. Oscar, with the electrified prongs in hand, stalked around her cage with two werewolves in tow on leashes. Beyond the walls of the house, she heard more werewolves clawing to get inside, chewing away at the wood. Her cage was even smaller than it was during her waking hours, and her three tormentors never wearied in their path around her.

Oscar struck the bars with his prongs, shooting electricity through them all around her. Mercy screamed in terror, finding it difficult to get the sound to emerge from her throat.

———————

"ROSE, GET OVER HERE."

Mercy awoke covered in sweat and panting in confusion. She looked around the room with a half-asleep weariness and rubbed at her eyes, urging herself to wake up. Something was happening and she needed to be awake to see what it was.

With shaky hands, she picked herself up off of the cold cage floor and looked toward the front door. Oscar paced back and forth before the door, his features a mixture of rage and terror. The clear fear on his face woke her up fully.

"What's taking you so long?" he cried, making Mercy jump. "This is not the time to be lollygagging! Get your butt over here!"

"Sorry, sir!" Rose called breathlessly from the back bedroom before rushing out to see him. She had changed into a thin linen gown that looked like a nightgown. Her natural hair was unwrapped and fell down to her shoulders. She didn't look scared as much as she looked antsy. "I'm sorry, sir. I had to prepare food for tomorrow and get changed, and it took longer than I—"

"Don't give me your ruddy excuses," he said. "The moon doesn't wait for anyone. You and I both know that. Now come on before we run out of time."

She gave a short nod and together they hurried out the front door. They were in such a rush that the door didn't close properly and Mercy pushed herself into a corner of her cage to watch through the open door.

It was late twilight, and the stars were beginning to emerge in the purple and pink sky. A cold breeze swept in and Mercy caught the scent of rain and fallen leaves on the breeze. It filled her with memories of playing outside, of helping her father chop wood, and of waiting on the ground for his truck to come home at dawn. It was a comfort, something she hadn't expected to feel after the brutality she had experienced earlier, and she was grateful for it.

"Come on, let's get you tethered out here so you don't kill yourself against the barricade in the night."

Oscar's words pulled Mercy from her memories. She

angled her head to see him picking up a heavy collar from the ground. As Oscar backed away from her, Rose lifted off her thin gown and stowed it in a metal container near the front door.

Mercy backed away for a moment for fear of Rose spotting her, then she leaned back in again when Rose left the front door. Oscar brought over a long, heavy chain and hooked it onto Rose's collar. Then he followed it to the end near the front door and hooked it on the wall there.

She couldn't see Rose anymore, but she could see Oscar struggle for a moment at the wall bracket. He hovered near the doorway, stepping slowly closer to get back inside. He clearly knew better than to get too close when Rose was so near the change.

"Go on," he said to her, "get out there. I don't want you changing at the front door again."

Mercy listened to Rose's footsteps as she walked further away from the house. A cold wind came again and Mercy shivered at the thought of having to walk out there naked.

Oscar tethered Rose for the night, closer to the front door than Mercy expected him to do it. Why was he risking her getting into the house by having her so close? Or maybe he had shot her as a transformed werewolf before too. Unlike the others outside, Rose wasn't dosed with Liquid Lead. Oscar seemed to understand the dangers of that. Mercy had seen real fear in his eyes when he had demanded Rose to get outside with him. Perhaps that was where his limp came from. The thought gave Mercy a small glimmer of hope.

"Keep going!" he called to Rose before holding up a hand. "That's good. I'll see you in the morning then, wolf," he said. Without another glance back, he limped back to the house and closed the door behind him. Mercy watched as he ensured every lock on the door was latched before he leaned his back on the door and took a deep, shuddering breath. He was shaking. That was definitely fear. He wasn't as impervious to fear as he liked to pretend.

It was encouraging. Mercy put the observation aside for later.

He turned away from the door and glanced at Mercy. "Werewolves are cowards when you know how to keep them in line." He unhooked the prongs from his belt and leaned it against the wall. "They fear anything silver." He put a sheathed blade on a side table. "But they cower under any threat of violence. Target their human side. That's the way to go. These hunters all get it wrong trying to tackle the beasts at night. Go during the day when they're soft and afraid. Humans are always easier to tame than beasts." He lifted his chin. "But I'm sure good old Solomon taught you that, didn't he, child?"

Mercy shook her head. Her father hadn't cared about werewolf interactions, only in how they killed humans. In fact, he never mentioned that they turned into humans during the day. Maybe he was afraid it would humanize them too much in her eyes. But in her father's eyes, once they transformed into bloodthirsty beasts, they were irredeemable.

Mercy had struggled to unlearn that lesson over the

years since his death. She sometimes still slid back into those false beliefs.

Oscar beamed with pride. "I didn't think so. Solomon only had money and murder on his mind." When he approached her cage, Mercy backed away, aware of how quickly he could get violent. She hadn't even known about the knife he kept on him until he put it on the table. What other kinds of weapons did he carry?

"There's no need to be frightened of me. I know it looks bad, but I promise I only have your best interests in mind. We talked about that, remember?" He pulled out a keyring from his pocket. "Of course, if you do try to attack me, I'll kill you in cold blood and nobody will know a damn thing." His eyes flashed to her, his expression blank. "Do you understand me?"

Mercy swallowed down the whimper trying to escape her throat. "I understand."

A woman's shrill scream made Mercy jump, and she looked toward the door. Rose was transforming already. Oscar hadn't been wrong about them running out of time. The two other werewolves howled, their voices mingling in an off-key chorus that made goose flesh crawl up Mercy's spine.

Oscar snorted a laugh. "Yeah, I guess there's no leaving tonight for you." He unlocked the padlock on Mercy's cage and pocketed it along with the keyring with unnerving calm. He might be terrified of Rose when she was transformed, but he didn't have any fear for Mercy. "Guess you're stuck with me instead for the night, child. Come on, I'll make us some dinner."

He turned his back to her and headed for the kitchen.

Mercy couldn't help but feel slightly outraged that he didn't fear her, wasn't even wary of her. But she wasn't a threat, was she? She had no more power than Rose had being leashed like a dog outside. If she tried anything, he could kill her. That wasn't an empty threat. Rose had made that clear. He had clearly killed others before her and even though he played nice around her, he could change his mind at any moment.

The only way to survive this was to play along, even if she hated every moment. Even if it felt like a horrible insult to her mother and father to do it here in her child-hood home.

Mercy pushed the cage door open and stepped out. She went to the dining table and sat down in one of the wooden chairs. Immediately, she noticed several changes Oscar had made. Almost every drawer and cabinet in the kitchen had been fixed with a padlock, some with different sizes, different shapes, and colors. That was why he needed a keyring. Oscar had a key for every one of them, making sure they were locked up at all times. What she wasn't sure about was if he had always had the kitchen like this or if this was a new change because Mercy was here.

Oscar was chopping up a pile of vegetables that he had fetched from some jars. None of them were in season, so he must have canned them months ago for use, or purchased them from others who had. Mercy had once helped manage a small farm on the grounds, but it only had herbs and a few tomatoes and potatoes.

It hadn't been much because she and her father weren't really farmers; they were trappers. They only had it to help cover the lean times. Usually her father brought groceries back when he went into town, so they didn't need the garden much, especially as the werewolf numbers got higher in the area. Oscar must have made some major changes in the backyard if he had the ability to can vegetables now.

"Did Solomon teach you how to cook?" Oscar asked, pouring the chopped vegetables into a pot.

Outside, the werewolves howled, a long, lonesome sound that made Mercy anxious. She had always associated the sound of howling werewolves with a threat. She had always heard them from a distance, not just outside the wall. Even at the mill, she hadn't heard them howl. It was going to be difficult to unlearn that reaction.

"Yes, sir," she said. "My dad taught me a lot of things. I know how to cook, bake, and—"

"I didn't ask for a list," he interrupted her. "I wasn't sure what kind of teaching he gave you, if any. Solomon never came across as much of a teacher to me." He picked up the pot with both hands and limped over to the fireplace. He hung the cast-iron pot with a hook before swinging it over the blaze. He tossed an extra log onto the fire, letting the flames and sparks fly up to the pot. He dragged his wooden chair over from her cage to the small dining table and settled down opposite her. "Your father didn't strike me as a man of many smarts. Sure, he could shoot well and trapped werewolves as well as any hunter, but maths and languages weren't exactly his forte, from what I could tell."

Mercy sat down opposite him with a glare. "My father had plenty of smarts," she grit out on instinct. She certainly didn't agree with everything her father did. He had far too many faults and was abusive as well as short-tempered, but he was not a kidnapper. He had taught her the best he knew how and even if he wasn't book smart, he had still protected her from a harsh world.

Oscar glared at her as he crossed his arms on top of the table. "Solomon knew how to catch and kill werewolves. I'll give him that. But not much else. Didn't have much appreciation for the arts except for the painting I did of your mother, but I think that's an exception." He chuckled. "The man didn't have much kindness in him, did he?"

His gaze bore into her and Mercy almost felt as if he could see through a lie before it even touched her tongue. It was as if he knew about the beatings she bore, the verbal lashings, and the many nights she cried herself asleep in bed. She looked away from him and shook her head, feeling guilty for alluding to her father's abuse but unable to lie about it.

"As I thought..." He sighed. "You seem like a child who has been beaten her whole life. Is that true?"

Her chest tightened at his question. The fact that he asked her so directly, here in the kitchen where she grew up, made it so much worse. She remembered vividly spilling a pot of hot water onto the floor when she was eight. It had been one of the first times she had been asked to cook dinner for the two of them. She had avoided getting burned, but she hadn't avoided the belt her father took to her backside when he saw what she had done. Her eyes lingered on the corner of the cabinets she had used to cower from him. The guilt still ate at her for making such a bad mistake.

Then she remembered her father was dead and a little flicker of joy sprang up—one she snuffed out quickly.

"Mercy?" Oscar pressed, pulling her back to the question.

"Not my entire life," she admitted, pushing down the shame. "He died a few years back."

He nodded sagely, as though he knew the answers to these questions already. "So not your whole life, just most of it." He eased back in his chair. "I'm sorry he put you through that."

Mercy scoffed. "Don't pretend to have pity for me when you're the one kidnapping people and trapping them here."

His smile fell to a pursed line and his gaze darkened. His hands balled into fists and Mercy half-expected to get hit, but instead he grunted and got to his feet. He went to grab a wooden cup, cracked open a barrel in the corner, and scooped out some amber liquid. "Want some?" he asked without turning toward her.

"No… thank you," she said. She didn't know what he was getting, but she could guess.

He wiped the cup down on a hanging towel, then returned to the table, settling down with a groan in the chair.

Despite how slowly he moved and the relatively lackadaisical attitude, the air still felt charged between them.

Mercy's heart pounded furiously in her chest. The man was dangerous, violent, and unpredictable. Her instincts screamed to get as far away from him as possible, but that wasn't an option. She was completely at his mercy in this place, and she hated it.

He took a leisurely drink from his glass before letting out a satisfied sigh. "It's always best to talk about such unpleasantness with a drink in hand." He slid a cup of water across the table to her. She glanced at it dubiously.

"It's not drugged, and it's not alcohol." He chuckled between sips of his drink. "Unlike you, I don't wander around with a bundle of needles in my pocket. Maybe some paralyzing powder, I'll admit, but I've already got you here, don't I? There's no need to be frightened of any food or water I give you now."

Mercy had reached for the cup of water but froze at his words. He had the injection needles that she had brought in her pouch with the cure she had created! She almost reached for her pouch to see if they were still there, but of course they weren't. They were gone along with the pouch. She also didn't want to give away how much that comment rattled her. He was clearly trying to poke and find weaknesses. Mercy had no intention of giving him anything—or at least as few as possible. He had an uncanny way of getting to her, and somehow he knew exactly what to say to make her talk. It was unnerving.

She drank from the cup while Oscar studied her closely. It made her skin crawl.

"You know..." A lop-sided smile came across Oscar's lips that made her uneasy. "Maybe I've been going about this all wrong. Maybe instead of me asking all the questions, you should get a few too." He rolled his shoulders, a mixture of a shrug and a stretch. "I'm sure you have something you want to ask me. So shoot, let's hear it."

She watched him carefully. "I do have a few, now that you mention it. Like why were you in Crowsmirth?"

His eyes glittered at the question. "I lost one of my werewolf guard dogs a week or so back. Missed having my trusty pair out there to keep trespassers at bay. They can be quite useful to have on hand, as you've seen. When I heard of the numbers expected in the werewolf assault, I thought it was a good time to visit that crumbling place again. Hunters talk, as you know, and everybody knew that place was going to bring in a pretty penny. I may not be into hunting werewolves as much as I used to, but I still know who to ask."

Mercy blinked. "But the inn. You had the keys to the room where we stayed overnight. How did you do that?"

Oscar chuckled. "The old innkeeper had been killed the previous night. Real bloodbath supposedly. Almost as bad as the night we met. I simply showed up and said I was his replacement." He put his cup on the table and grinned. "They were all too focused on the werewolves. Nobody seemed to care if I was telling the truth or not, which suited me just fine. Not that I think they would have cared a dime if I was caught in a lie. So many people were happy to have a place to sleep for the night, nobody asked who I even was." He gestured to the front of the house. "I found Jamison out there feasting on the old innkeeper's remains right behind my desk. Can you believe the luck? He practically dropped in my lap!" He laughed, "Of course, I set the bait by pulling the old innkeeper's remains out of the back room to draw them inside. Seemed to do the trick nicely! You saw old Jamison feasting on his body at the entrance, right?"

Mercy shuddered at the memory. "So you just impersonated someone and led the werewolves right into the inn? And you robbed anybody who wanted to stay the night." She winced at the realization. "So many people died there that night."

"Yeah, pity that. Though you have to admit, they were pretty foolish to think that staying in an inn would keep them safe from a hundred werewolves, right?" He laughed, "As long as I pretended I knew what I was doing, nobody suspected a thing. People want normalcy when surrounded by chaos, and I was happy to give them that delusion." He leaned forward over the table, the foam from his drink clinging to his stubble. "Isn't that how you've been getting by? Where was it, Farrell Mill, you said you were from? Clearly you've been pretending to be somebody else too, taking on a disguise that wasn't you. I'm sure you've been out there pretending like you weren't holed up here your whole life. Can't really blame you there."

Mercy clenched her jaw to keep from saying too much. He knew far more about her than she knew about him and if she rose to his bait, she would still be in the dark. He was good at trying to misdirect her. She just had to keep her cool and stay focused. It wasn't easy.

Problem was she didn't know what to ask next. It

would be easy to go down the questions he clearly wanted her to ask so he could try to get information out of her. She had so many questions before, but now all she could think of was Farrell Mill and Andrei, who had no idea where she was or what had happened to her. Then there was Kit, who was so scared of messing up back at the inn. Mercy knew she had probably not taken Mercy's disappearance well. And Leyda didn't know Rose wasn't dead. What if she did something horrible because she didn't know? What would happen with the research with Thomas?

Mercy took a deep breath to calm herself.

Oscar arched his eyebrows. "Is that it then? Not nearly as many questions as I expected. Hmm, perhaps you didn't inherit your mother's inquisitiveness like I had suspected." He leaned back in his chair, a smile on his lips. "Such a disappointment. But it isn't your fault. You can't help who raised you, and you certainly can't help where you end up." Another chuckle as he sipped his drink. She wanted to slam his face into the table.

No, that wasn't a good idea. She needed to prove she was at his level, that she was more than her rage and her abuse. She tore her gaze away from him and looked into the fireplace, desperate for anything to jog her mind. While her gaze lingered over the embers and flames, the smell of cooked vegetables made her stomach growl. No, focus. She looked around at the stone hearth and finally met the cheerful gaze of her mother in the portrait. Her smile made the tightness in Mercy's chest loosen and a calm focus fell over her, just as it used to when she looked at it.

Oscar scooted his chair backwards with a squeak and got to his feet. He had probably written her off as not worth his time, which was dangerous. If she wasn't worth Oscar's time, she imagined he was already planning on a way to get rid of her, as he did with the werewolf that used to be in Jamison's position. Mercy needed to capture his attention if she wanted to prove she was worthy of keeping around. Prove she was useful, even if it was just a farce.

"You knew my mother," Mercy stated calmly.

His smile flickered with a strained expression. "Yes, I did, as I told you earlier."

It was Mercy's turn to gloat. "It's my turn to ask questions, so tell me: how did you know her? Clearly, she wasn't interested in you like she was my father."

The strain in his smile shifted swiftly to a scowl. "That wasn't the case at all!"

In his rage, the wooden cup fell from his fingers and clattered to the floor. Mercy jumped. Oscar winced and closed his eyes, clearly working to compose himself. She waited in stunned silence.

Oscar had shown his rage over Mercy's father earlier when he had spoken about the painting, but she hadn't expected him to react so quickly when she brought up the topic. His clear distress at just mentioning it confirmed he was clearly still angry about it almost fifteen years later. She would have to tread cautiously. She didn't want to push him too hard or else she could be the target of that rage, whether it was at the end of a pair of prongs or a shot with a gun. Mercy didn't have

Rose's healing abilities. If he lost his temper at her, Mercy wasn't sure she would survive.

"Damn age getting to me," he muttered. Stooping down he snatched up the empty cup and dropped it into the wash basin.

Mercy fought the urge to roll her eyes at his excuse. She had seen his speed. She wasn't sure how old he was, but that didn't slow him down in the least. It was just like the inn where he allowed people to underestimate him. He wanted people to think of him as an old, feeble man when he was clearly stronger and faster than he looked. Oscar fetched another cup of ale before settling down across from her again.

"Your mother was a beautiful woman, both inside and out—a rare feat in these places. She knew how to turn her anger on and off as needed, could go from a rampage to a sweet muse in the blink of an eye. She had wit and charm to boot. Could make me laugh so hard I had tears in my eyes. Remarkable woman. Damn, I miss her." He held up his cup in a toast. "To you, my dear Anna, wherever you may be." He took a long gulp.

Mercy wanted to gag. She had a hard time believing her mother was as perfect as he made her out to be, or that she would give this creep the time of day. Not to mention the nerve of toasting her memory while he kept her only child kidnapped and threatened to shoot her. Oscar had a strong disconnect with reality, and once again Mercy found herself questioning what few facts he had given her.

She took a deep breath to focus herself and chose

her words carefully. "So, when did she leave you to be with my dad?"

The intense glare he gave made Mercy wish she had chosen her words better.

"Anna was too smitten by your father's dangerous nature to give me a proper chance. But oh, I tried!" He nodded at the portrait that hung above the fireplace. "The painting I made for her? I gifted it to them both as a wedding present."

Mercy nodded. He had told her this before, but apparently liked to repeat it. It was a strange claim to fame, but she wasn't going to stop him from continuing.

He put an arm over the back of his chair. His face was a little red from his drink. He gave a hearty nod. "I spent months on it. She would come by my home three times a week and pose for me. Those mornings became precious to me." He rubbed at his nose as his eyes glazed over with memory. "You see, Anna was sick of me tagging around all the time. She was tired of me always coming by her pub to talk. Said I caused trouble, such nonsense. All I wanted was for her to give me ten minutes of her time. Is that so much to ask?"

He let out a heavy sigh and looked down into his cup. "Then I heard she got engaged to that jerk Solomon."

"You were angry," Mercy said.

He gave a short nod, his jaw clenched. "I told her I couldn't let her go. I couldn't sleep knowing that brute was with her. I thought if I could show her the kind of person I was, prove to her I was worthy, she would see the real me. She would understand everything I had done was for her. She would finally see the truth."

To Mercy's shock, Oscar's eyes misted over. She waited a moment before prompting for an answer she felt was obvious. This clearly rattled him, and Mercy hoped she wasn't pushing him too far. "So, how did that work out?"

He let out a long sigh that smelled of rank ale. "Well, for one, she loved the painting. She couldn't stop herself from telling everyone she could about my talent. Even tried to get others to hire me to do paintings for them too." He made an annoyed sound. "I appreciated her support, but that wasn't what I wanted. That wasn't why I painted it. I didn't care about the money, and she knew that. It was all a game to her."

He turned the cup around in circles in his hands.

"I wanted her to see reason. I wanted her to see more than that smug hunter's face. I wanted her to see me, to understand my love for her." His voice grew louder as he continued. "I wanted her to see what all of Kanta understood—that Solomon Pinkerton would be the death of her. And sure as the gods spit on us, it's true. She only lasted one year after their wedding." He slammed a hand down on the table. "One year!"

Mercy jumped. She regretted taking him down this path. She shouldn't have provoked him. Her parents might be dead and beyond his wrath, but here she sat, the evidence of their relationship that he so hated. Mercy's very presence was proof of her parents' love for each other. Drawing attention to that wasn't a good idea.

Oscar laughed, and that was somehow worse than his rage. "Solomon hated that painting when I presented it to them on their wedding day. He hated that it was made by my hand, that his beloved wife had spent so much time with me so I could make it. I think he always suspected we were together, but Solomon probably suspected others too. He was always so damn paranoid. Suspicious of anything that dared to look at him or his wife."

Oscar laughed again and got to his feet, stalking over to the painting with that speed she had seen before. Part of her worried he would damage it. "You can imagine my shock to find it here, hung in the man's very home, in a place of reverence. All that venom he said to me about it years ago forgotten, I guess. He wanted to pay me to take it back, to burn it, he said—the nerve! But I refused. And then he hung it here to look at every day. His mind baffles me even still."

This was a crucial moment, Mercy realized. She either associated herself with her father and was treated with that same hostility, or she reminded him she was her mother's daughter too, and try her best to gain his trust. She needed that if she was going to escape. Even if it was a small and tenuous trust, she needed something that would keep him from pointing guns at her every few minutes. She needed to stay alive long enough to plan a way out.

"I always liked that painting," she said in a small voice. Oscar looked at her as if she was lying. She needed to do more.

Mercy got to her feet and joined him at the painting.

Her mother smiled down at her with mirth in her eyes, an unspoken joke on her lips. In retrospect, it was a strange visage to see her so cheerful when the world was overrun with werewolves and human trafficking. It was almost an idealized view of her rather than a true vision. Mercy always thought it reflected simpler times, an age before werewolves lurked in the shadows at night. But now she realized Kanta hadn't changed that much. The werewolves ruled the night, but the city was the same. The painting was a colorful interpretation of the truth.

Her mother wasn't a mischievous pub owner concealing a secret, but she wasn't the opposite of her father's cruelty either. She was merely a person who did the best she could with what she had. There was something achievable in that, a pair of shoes that weren't impossible to fill. She had been a person with wishes, wants, and fears, just like Mercy. She took a risk, and it ended up killing her in the end, but at least it had been her choice. At least she had chosen what she wanted to do with her life and had done it. Mercy only got a taste of that freedom at Farrell Mill, and she was determined to get it back.

"My father told me she died having me," Mercy stated, changing the subject down a more careful path. "The doctor gave her a choice: get rid of me and live, or keep me and risk her life. She lost that gamble. I'm sorry I lost my mother, but I'm so grateful to her for giving me the chance to live."

Oscar put a hand on her shoulder and it took all the willpower in her body not to pull away from him. She couldn't help but think of the powder he put on her in

Crowsmirth. She didn't want to be drugged again, but she also needed to gain his trust while he was willing to give it.

"Her death wasn't your fault," Oscar said.

There had been a time in her life when she would have loved to hear her father say those words to her. It hurt to know he never had. "I know," she said automatically, even though she wasn't sure if she meant it.

"I bet your old man blamed you still, didn't he?" Oscar didn't wait for her to respond. "That jerk was always looking for his next grudge. Well, he's dead now and good riddance."

Mercy felt frozen inside. Was she happy her father was dead? No, she felt terrible about it still. Why was he twisting around her words? Worse yet, why was there a kernel of truth to them?

"Solomon is no longer the man of the house, you hear me? I am. And as such, one of my first rules is you don't have to pretend to have liked him anymore. You can be honest with yourself. Admit that you hated him for how he treated you."

Mercy stood mute, her emotions battling within until she couldn't hold back the tempest any longer. "But I love him still, even though he's gone. He's my father." She should have stopped. She knew it was a terrible idea to continue, but she couldn't help it. Something had been released inside of her and she couldn't reel it back in again. "Dad was right. Mom died because of me and he did too. If I hadn't been born, they would still be alive today."

Oscar studied her with a dark gaze.

Hot tears streaked down Mercy's cheeks, but she barely noticed them. All of her grand plans to hold it in, to not show any weakness, to be some kind of statue in front of Oscar, crumbled to pieces. She stood vulnerable before him and she no longer cared.

"You act like I should hate my father and I know he wasn't perfect, but he was a decent man. He didn't deserve to be eaten by werewolves. They never buried his body either. We had no funeral. He didn't deserve that. He deserved to be laid to rest beside my mother!"

Her voice broke, and she started openly crying in front of this man who would kill her if he felt like it. The logical, strategic part of her mind screamed at her to stop. She couldn't let her emotions pour out like this. It was all weakness he would use against her somehow. But Mercy couldn't stop. Talking about her parents here in her own home, the place she never wanted to return to again, was simply too much. The memories of her father's cruelty alongside his kindness and finally his horrible death were just too much.

Oscar let out a sigh and wrapped an arm around her, trying to pull her into a hug. "Come here, child. There's no need for all that."

"No!" Mercy shouted, which caused Oscar to back off. "You don't put your hands on me again. You brought me here to this place—I never wanted to come back here! I never wanted to be reminded of living here ever again."

She trailed off into sobs and backed up to the wall beside the fireplace, her head knocking against the frame of her mother's painting. Mercy couldn't look up into her smiling face again. Instead, she sank down to the floor and pulled her knees up, as tears continued to fall.

Oscar crouched down opposite her. "Hey, look at me," he urged.

Mercy shook her head and bit her lip.

"I'm not going to hurt you. Just look at me, damn it."

With a sniff, Mercy looked up at his bloodshot eyes, feeling like she had finally fallen into a thousand little pieces. All the bravado, the acts she put on, all of her attempts to look like she knew what she was doing crumbled. This was all that was left, a terrified, sobbing child who missed her mom and dad terribly.

"You can love your old man, but still accept that he hurt you, okay?"

Mercy blinked at him. "What?"

Oscar shook his head. "That old goat really did a number on you, didn't he, child?"

She turned away from him, but he took hold of her chin and forced her to look back at him. She didn't have the strength to fight him.

"Your dad? He's gone. I'm your new dad now. You're my daughter, understood?"

Mercy didn't fully understand what he meant or why he was so determined to perform this play, but she knew she had to respond regardless. She had to struggle to nod around his grip.

"Good. See, we're going to do things a little differently now. You'll see that your father's abuse can't hurt you anymore. You'll be free of him. Together we'll make new memories in this haunted house of yours. And maybe, just maybe, you'll see I'm not the bad guy you think I am."

He released her chin. Her mouth hurt from the pressure of his fingers. Oscar probably did believe he was telling the truth, that he would somehow prove that he was a better dad than her father had been. But Mercy could already see where this sick game was going and part of the reason she couldn't stop crying was because she couldn't stand the thought of living in this house with a violent man for a second time. At least she had understood her father's quirks and demands. At least she could follow his rules and knew he loved her at the end of the day. This man would kill her if she refused. That had been made clear as soon as she stepped outside. But for some crazy reason, he really did believe he could be a better father.

All the pain and heartache was coming back to her in a tumult, only this time she would have the dangers of free roaming werewolves to deal with on top of Oscar's angry outbursts. Had this attempt to gain his trust and somehow learn a path to escape worked in her favor at all, or had it completely backfired? Maybe this was all a grand ruse on Oscar's part to break her down completely. If that was the case, it had certainly succeeded.

4

CHANGING PATTERNS

THEY ATE IN SILENCE. The simple vegetable meal was a little bland and needed salt, but Mercy was grateful to eat real food. Rose had given her oatmeal to eat that morning, but it simply hadn't lasted long enough. Oscar had piled her plate high with food as though aware she must be starving.

After dinner, Oscar clutched a pipe between his teeth. The woodsy smell of the smoke tickled her nose. He stared out the back window at the dark forest in the distance. The roar of crickets only occasionally was interrupted by the howls of the three werewolves outside and mingled with others in the distance. Even with their attempt to clear out the pack in Kanta, there were more werewolves in these woods. All close enough to communicate with Silver, Jamison, and Rose outside.

Oscar was a dangerous mystery, one she knew she had to untangle if she hoped to escape. Yes, he was obsessed with her mom and this strange desire to prove he was a better father figure than her dad had been, but that didn't give her much of an advantage. It only made her options complicated.

She finished her meal and eyed the kitchen counter. Oscar had put dozens of locks on all the cabinets, but maybe some he had left unlocked. Perhaps she could take her dish over and find the soap somewhere. Maybe she could clean her own dish like she used to when she lived here.

Mercy got to her feet. Oscar didn't take his gaze off the open window. She picked up her dish and stepped around the table. Before she could reach the wash basin, Oscar had a hand wrapped around her wrist. Pain pulsed through her arm and she gasped in surprise.

"What are you doing?" His grumble made it sound as though he was coming out of a daze.

Mercy struggled to form words through her hoarse throat. "Cleaning up. I used to clean up my dishes all the time before."

He met her gaze, and Mercy's heart skipped a beat. He glanced down at the plate in her hands then up to her again.

"Leave it." He hadn't let go of her wrist.

"It's just a dirty plate, it won't take me a moment to—"

Far faster than she expected, he flung her backward. The wooden plate fell from her fingers and broke into several pieces on the floor. Mercy fell with it, hitting the floor hard on her elbows. Large splinters flew across the floor and a few bounced up, scraping her cheeks.

Oscar towered over her, chest heaving and hands splayed at his sides. "Now look at the mess you've made.

I said no, child. Didn't you hear me? It isn't a debate. It isn't an option. It's the final word."

Mercy was too breathless to respond. Her eyes welled with tears but she fought against them. Her elbows throbbed. Her cheeks stung. She berated herself. He was too volatile to sneak around; she had known this already. So why had she tried to go back to normalcy again? There was no returning to that, and she knew it.

He stalked around the kitchen, running a hand through his hair. "Rose isn't going to be happy having so much to clean up come dawn."

Mercy glanced down at the wooden splinters of her dish. One large piece caught her eye. It had broken at a point sharp enough to do some real damage. With a deep breath, she reached for it and tucked it into her pocket so quickly she hoped she wasn't seen.

Oscar continued his lumbering pace, back and forth, as if he was truly worried about what Rose would think in the morning. Maybe he had drunk too much. Or maybe she had pushed him too far.

Slowly she got to her feet, wary and determined not to be taken by surprise again. When he still didn't look at her, she realized she would have to speak up.

"Where should I stay tonight? Back in the cage?"

He stared at her for a long moment, so she spoke up again.

"I want to go to bed." It wasn't a lie either. She was exhausted and wanted to be left alone.

Briefly he looked ready to toss her around the room again, then his expression shifted and he chuffed a laugh. "Of course not. You're my daughter. You go to your room."

Mercy wasn't sure if she heard him right. "My room?"

"Sure." He smiled and picked up his pipe to puff on. "You do remember where your room is, right?"

She gave a short nod then headed toward the hallway with the two bedrooms. Her elbows and face hurt, and she was grateful to get away from him. She paused before going down the hall, placing a hand on the wooden wall and remembering the years long gone. Her father rushing out late at night to hunt werewolves. Mercy making sure everything was clean and ready for his return. So many years spent in this hall hurrying across the floorboards, she had never imagined the changes that would come.

Rose had been rushing between the bedrooms that morning, gathering laundry and changing linens. It might have been Mercy's room once upon a time, but now it seemed like it belonged to either Oscar or Rose. No, Oscar would have taken her father's room, of course. Just like he was trying to take his daughter.

She glanced back at Oscar. He stood in the kitchen, his pipe sat smoldering on its side on the countertop. Both of his hands clung to his scalp as he stared down at the mess on the floor.

Mercy swallowed down her nerves then asked, "Isn't Rose staying in my room?"

He spun around, arms dropping back to his sides as if he hadn't just been worrying about something. "You're concerned about Rose? She'll be fine. It's not like she needs a bed at night." He grinned as if it was a joke. Mercy had seen firsthand how brutal a werewolf transformation could be. That was not a joke.

"Okay," she said, and turned to head back.

"Mercy?"

Just hearing him call out her name made her body go cold. She stiffened and turned around slowly toward him, afraid of what was coming next.

"Tomorrow will be different. We start over, okay?"

She looked at him in confusion.

"No more fighting. Tomorrow, you're my daughter and I'm your father. Understood?"

Mercy wanted to laugh in his face. Instead she nodded, knowing full well that when morning came, Oscar would be just as much of a monster. Time alone wouldn't fix him, and neither would promises. In fact, based on what she had learned from dealing with monsters all her life, it might make him worse.

———————

BIRDSONG LILTED in through the shuttered windows. Mercy turned over in her bed, briefly thinking she was alone at home again. Then the ugly truth from the previous night returned to her like a cold blanket wrapped around her insides. Her elbows and cheeks stung as she came fully awake. She could hear the huffs of the tied up werewolves in the yard and someone was working in the kitchen. Water was sloshing around somewhere.

If only she was alone, then living in this place would be so much easier.

The sunlight that seeped in through the cracks in the shutters was far too bright. She blinked and looked around the room in the morning light, but she didn't recognize her own room. Outfits she had never worn hung on the wall. A couple of pairs of worn-out work boots covered in mud sat by the door. The smell of brimstone lingered beneath the sweet scent of morning. The childhood bedroom she remembered so fondly was gone completely.

This was no longer her room or even her home. It hadn't been hers for a long time either, maybe even a year. She had never really liked the house, but seeing how different her childhood bedroom was, the place she had grown up since she was a baby, she felt violated. She hadn't given this private space of hers over to anyone, and she certainly hadn't wanted anyone else to see the house she had shared with her father. Yet it had happened regardless. Why did she care now? She hadn't cared until she was forced to come back.

Perhaps she should have come back home earlier if she wanted to keep this piece of her life intact. She certainly had time to since she had stayed at Farrell Mill. But no, she wasn't sure if she would have ever wanted to. It had been easier to lose herself in her new life than to linger over the charred remains of her old one. She had a bad habit of wanting to let the bad memories of her past be left for nature to reclaim. The same as the werewolf cage they had found in the woods. There was something so freeing about that. But that wasn't what happened here.

Oscar clearly knew if Mercy was alive that she wouldn't want to come back to her childhood home. He must have been banking on it. She suspected that's one of the reasons he chose her old home as a base. It was an insult to her father and to honor her mother, as gross as that actually sounded. Mercy was an unexpected accident, unfortunately for her.

Her elbows and knees throbbed as she got out of bed. Her cheeks still stung but not nearly as badly. Her elbows were bruised from falling on them last night, and her knees were still bruised from falling into the dirt at Crowsmirth when Oscar drugged her. He called it paralyzing powder, and it certainly did just that. Three wounds from the man who wanted to be her father, not counting the bruising she probably had on her cheeks from him grabbing her chin last night. It made her clench her teeth together.

Last night she had gambled and mostly lost. She tried to outsmart Oscar, but he ended up outmaneuvering her each and every time. She thought back to his stricken expression in the kitchen before she had headed to bed, his hands gripping at his scalp and hair. He was losing control of himself too. She had caused that.

Mercy smirked. Maybe last night wasn't a total loss. She could get under his skin.

Oscar hadn't intended to lose control. He had struck out at her for no good reason, with her wanting to clean her dish. That's why he wanted to start over today. His temper was the key. That's what made him unpredictable, but it also made him dangerous.

She sighed as she straightened the bed and did her best to make herself feel more put together. Anger was Oscar's weakness, but it was Mercy's too. She had never reacted well to someone losing their temper around her. She tended to shut down, mentally distance herself. It was a way to survive, yes, but she needed to keep her head. She wouldn't be able to do anything if she froze like a prey animal every time he got mad. In fact, that could make things worse.

Mercy reached into her pocket and pulled out the splinter from the shattered plate. Her leg still hurt from sleeping with it on her, but she hadn't dared trying to do anything with it last night. Oscar was too on edge and unpredictable. Today was different.

She reached behind the headboard of her bed and felt the empty knot in the wood. It was dusty. Good, maybe they hadn't found her hiding spot yet. She reached a finger inside the hole, looped it around, and pulled. The tiny square piece of wood fell easily out of her headboard and into her palm.

Eyes glued to the door, she waited. No footsteps sounded, only water being sloshed around in the kitchen. Holding her breath, she slid the splinter inside and popped on the lid.

Good, it was hidden. At some point, she would need to examine her hiding place closer to see if anything useful was in there. For now, she would have to wait and play Oscar's sick game.

She just had to be smart and not lose her head again

like last night. Though Oscar could be thinking the same thing too.

———

THE HALLWAY WAS empty when Mercy stepped out of her room. Oscar's bedroom door was ajar, and she poked her head in for a quick glance. Padlocks on the end tables. That wasn't surprising, but it still made her angry. She looked around and saw Oscar wasn't in the room. She dropped down to check under the bed, but there was nothing. The thin closet door had another padlock. How many locks did he have on hand, anyway?

With a sigh, Mercy made her way down the hallway and back to the open living space with her cage and the kitchen. Morning sunshine came in through the window and she could hear the birds chirping outside. It gave a strange mood of happiness to the place, even though she knew she was a prisoner here.

Rose stood at the kitchen counter. Two buckets of water sat at her feet—one soapy and one clean. A pile of dirty dishes sat on one counter beside a clean stack of washed dishes. She had a drying cloth in hand and was wiping a plate, probably one used last night. The mess Mercy had made from dropping her plate last night had been completely swept up. Even the pieces that had flown halfway across the room had been cleaned. Mercy felt bad.

As she hovered in the doorway from the hallway, Mercy said, "Good morning."

Rose glanced up at her, exhaustion etched on her

face. Deep bags hung beneath her bloodshot eyes, and she turned back to her work without a word.

Mercy pursed her lips. That was fair. Mercy had gotten her electrocuted by talking to her the other day. She didn't want to risk getting her hurt again. She considered her words more carefully before speaking again.

"Where is he?"

This time, she didn't look up from her work.

"In the garden out back," Rose said. "One of the few places he doesn't keep a werewolf tethered." She wiped at her mouth with the back of her arm. Her hand was shaking. "Not yet, at least."

That was a useful piece of information Mercy hadn't expected from her. Maybe Rose wasn't that mad at her after all. Maybe she was merely stressed out and tired. Completely understandable, considering she had to pick up all the time and follow Oscar's orders.

Mercy stepped into the room and sat down at the dining table. "I'm sorry I took your room last night."

Rose shrugged.

Mercy sighed and tried again. "Do you want me to finish washing and putting away those dishes away while you get some sleep?"

Rose gaped at her. "You would do that? For me?"

Mercy nodded, lowering her voice. "I know how painful the transformation can be every night. And I also got you hurt yesterday. I'm sorry about that. You need to sleep and recover while you can. Especially in the morning when the transformation back is so fresh. Let me take care of this. You go get some sleep."

Mercy rolled up her sleeves and got to her feet. Rose glanced toward the back window once as though she expected Oscar's face to appear. After a beat, Rose flung down the rag and hurried down the hall past Mercy.

As she passed, she whispered, "Thank you." Mercy could see tears in her eyes.

Only once she saw the bedroom door close did she enter the kitchen. The drying cloth had seen better days with long pieces of thread hanging off of it. Once upon a time Mercy would have been in charge of repairing it and keeping it intact for just a little longer. She and her father were always trying to make everything last as long as possible. The wooden plateware consisted of the same pieces Mercy had grown up with and she had to push away the pang of nostalgia at drying them again, just as she had as a child.

She didn't need to think about her father bringing home a new set when she was eight, or the cups he told her had been her mother's favorite. Those had a lovely red color. All the wooden pieces had deep cracks in them, especially the plates, from too much washing and not enough oils. Her father had taught her how to make things last, and seeing the mistreatment of the simple plates and cups broke her heart more than she expected. Not that it was Rose's fault. No, Mercy blamed Oscar for all of this.

Mercy glanced out the back window to see rows upon rows of vegetables. The trees beyond the fence had started to fade from a bright orange to a dull brown. Winter would be coming soon. Mercy didn't know a lot about gardening, but she did know there was a lot left to harvest and little time to do it. Soon, the snow would come and bury anything not already plucked from the ground. If Oscar was planning on living here over winter, they would need food to eat.

She had assumed Oscar had to have lived here for months based on the tethered werewolf bodyguards and the state of the wooden plateware. Oscar was clearly not buying new plates or cups for them to use when he went into town, and nothing was being properly taken care of, everything was getting worn out. It surprised her only how quickly improper care could cause damage.

Oscar had probably planted a bunch of seeds and prepared the earth properly so it would all grow, but he clearly had overestimated on how quickly he could harvest everything. Especially with his bad leg. He would need help. That might allow Mercy to get a better view of the backyard.

Mercy washed a plate, stacked it, and then picked up the next. Being held captive was dangerous enough, but knowing her captor had no clue how to grow his own food and was more focused on servants than survival made her anxious.

If Oscar got desperate enough for money, would he sell Mercy to another trafficker? Carter once boasted she would make a pretty penny on the market, and that wasn't something she liked to think about. But she guessed Oscar had likely considered it, since he was so familiar with that business.

She took a deep breath and started on the next plate. This situation got more and more nerve-wracking.

5

A DUTIFUL DAUGHTER

MERCY STEPPED OUT the backdoor into a rush of frigid wind sweeping through the field, causing her to shiver. The bright blue sky had few clouds. Brown leaves fell from the trees in droves, carpeting the grounds. Autumn would soon be over and winter was already promising to be intense. She closed the door behind her and shoved her hands into her pockets. Already she second-guessed her decision to come outside. Then she spotted Oscar.

Peeling off his work gloves, he stood beside a pile of freshly harvested butternut squash. He glared at her and even though he hadn't taken a step toward her, Mercy started backing away toward the door. Oscar had a menace about him that made her instinctively shrink away. She had seen he could be surprisingly fast. She recalled the speed with which he had grabbed her wrist the night before, going from sitting and enjoying his pipe to suddenly standing beside her and holding her arm. Mercy gripped the handle of the door, ready to flee back inside the house again if she had to.

Oscar didn't stalk toward her or raise his voice. Somehow that made it worse. Her instincts screamed at her to return to the safety of the house, but there was no obvious threat. Mercy took a deep, steadying breath and forced herself to hold her ground. If she wanted to escape this place, her old home now turned into a nightmare, she would have to chance leaving the house, facing the man and the monster who kept her here. To hide would be to give in to this fate. If he could make her so terrified without saying a word or raising a hand, then she had already lost.

"Why are you out here?" Oscar's calm voice warned of a torrent if he became displeased with her response.

Mercy jumped when he spoke and chided herself for it. "I saw you were working in the garden."

He glanced at her and then turned back to his worktable. "And?"

Unclenching her fingers from the doorknob took effort, but walking the few steps toward him made her break out into a sweat despite the crisp air. He was training her to be terrified of him and it was working. She needed to fight against her instincts.

"It's almost winter and there is still a lot to do."

She walked up beside his worktable and noted the enormous blade on the far end. It was far larger than the knife she had seen on him the night before. Did he have that on him last night too?

She forgot her train of thought for a moment and had to catch it again before she could continue. Oscar was organizing the small harvest he had gathered. He still hadn't looked at her again, and it felt like a warning. In fact, everything he did felt like a warning to her frazzled nerves.

"I thought I could help you gather vegetables and put them into storage. Do you have a cellar you're using or—"

"No, I don't think I need your help with any of this." He rested his hand down beside the blade and glanced at her. "I need to know I can trust you first, and you haven't done a damn thing to gain my trust yet, have you?"

Mercy swallowed down the dryness in her throat as the wind died down completely. The silence left behind was loud. There weren't even birds chirping in the trees. "I want to try to earn your trust," Mercy lied. She steeled herself for saying the word that hurt her most. "Father." Saying it tasted like poison on her tongue.

He smirked. "I appreciate the effort, but your scowl tells me all the truth I need to know." Sadness flickered across his face briefly before he wiped it clean with stony disapproval. He placed his hand on the handle of the blade. "I thought we were both going to give this father-daughter business a shot, but maybe you're not that interested. Maybe you truly are beyond my help."

Alarm bells screamed in Mercy's head, but she refused to flee. She rooted her feet to the ground. "You haven't given me an opportunity. I want to give this a shot, but you have to give me a chance."

She hated how desperate she sounded, but pushed on regardless.

"I just got here a couple of days ago. My fath—"
She stopped herself, corrected, and continued,
"Solomon and I had years together. Most of my life.
And we butt heads all the time. If you could have seen
some of the fights we had, maybe you would understand
why this is so difficult for me."

He looked at her, clearly listening. Good. Whatever
it took to keep him from looking at that damn blade.

"I just see you doing all this work, and I know we
need this food to survive the winter. I'm not used to just
sitting around. I want to help… Pa." The word still
tasted bitter to say, but somehow it was better than referring to him using the same word when she spoke of her
real father.

He gave a small smile. "Pa. I like the sound of that."

"I can't just sit around and do nothing while you
work yourself to the bone in this cold. Let me help you."

She knew better than to approach him this time.
She'd made that mistake last night. She also chose not to
mention Rose. The less she brought his attention to her,
the better. So she kept this focused on the two of them.
Feeding into his sick delusion might help her gain just a
little more freedom and hopefully a little more time. It
was a dangerous risk, and she had to pretend to be
friendly so he would let his guard down. She had no
idea if he truly believed her, but if he did, maybe a
small glimmer of hope existed that she could get out of
here.

"I guess it makes sense. No child of mine is content
to sit around and be waited on all day long."

Mercy allowed herself a small sigh of relief. Then

she gestured with an open hand out to the garden. "So you'll let me help?"

"Yes," he said with a bemused expression. "I think it'll give you character. I think you'd do well to get back to some chores around the house. Might make it feel a bit more homey for you."

"That's it exactly!" She nodded and pointed to a patch of greenery way in the back. "I thought I could start with those vegetables in the back and work my way forward. Looks like those are potatoes, I think, right? I've got some experience with those."

Oscar cut her off, wrapping a hand around her wrist. Forcibly he lowered her arm. Just like last night. Mercy's stomach dropped, but she didn't fight against him. Instead she stared at him with wide, fearful eyes.

He held onto her wrist and lifted the blade with his other hand. "No more of that. You aren't going anywhere near the fence without me, child. It's too dangerous out there. Too many things that could get you hurt and we don't want that. Understood?"

He dropped the blade to his side. Mercy felt a hot tear streak down her cheek.

"Yes, Pa."

"Good. I'm not a fan of punishing children, but I won't hesitate if you disobey me. Do I make myself clear, child?"

"Yes, Pa. Absolutely."

"I'm glad to hear it. That's the kind of positive, well-behaved attitude I want to see more of in you." He let go of her wrist and Mercy let it fall flat against her leg. Fear and adrenaline coursed through her. "Now, as for what you can do around here, I have a few ideas. But one is an absolute necessity. If we're going to trust one another, I think it's important to start with a big responsibility. That way you have no doubt I trust you. Agreed?"

She nodded, not quite sure what he was implying.

He cocked his head to the side. "I didn't hear you, child."

"Yes, Pa!" she said.

"Much better. Come with me. I think I have the perfect task for you."

Oscar kept the blade in his hand while he led her around the back of the house. He could talk about trust all day long, but that blade spoke his true feelings. From his body language to his words, everything was a threat. It was clear he knew that too.

Mercy followed him, still feeling the phantom of his grip around her wrist. Her stomach tied up in knots. If she didn't play along, she didn't doubt for a second Oscar would do far worse than frighten her. He didn't make idle threats.

THE MORNING SUN was blinding as they went around the side of the house toward the front yard. It took a moment for Mercy to be able to see properly around the sunlight gleaming around Oscar's limping, shadowy form ahead of her. She followed slowly, happy to use the sun to get some distance between them.

"Would you look at that? Guess we're getting some

meat on the table tonight." Oscar diverted toward the fence and away from the house.

Mercy wasn't sure if she was supposed to follow him or not since his speech earlier. So she stayed put. It took her a moment to figure out what he was even talking about. She didn't see any game around. Then, at the far end near the fence, she spotted a square-shaped cage covered in branches and leaves. She thought it was a pile of debris formed by the wind, but as she got a little closer, the glint of metal caught her eye along with a gray fluffy tail that waved in the breeze.

"What is it?" she asked, almost afraid to know.

"Two squirrels!" He said as he unlatched the cage and lifted the two motionless bodies into the air. "Looks like one got trapped, and the other died trying to rescue them." He chuckled as he stared at them, holding their faces close, as if passing judgment. "Couple of foolish creatures, if you ask me. So hellbent on saving someone they died." He looked up at her with a wicked smile. "Squirrels, right?"

Mercy grimaced at the thought. It was bad enough he held the two corpses with a strange glee instead of as a necessary cruelty to eat. But did he have to ridicule them after they died?

His eyes turned to her with that coldness that made her curl inward.

"You eat squirrels, oh daughter of mine?"

She blinked, not sure what to say. "I mean, if you need me to, sure."

"Doesn't matter if you do or don't." He gave her a wide grin. "One for us and the other for my pets. Here."

He tossed a squirrel at her and Mercy had to restrain herself from acting on instinct and trying to catch it. "You hold on to that one. This one is for the pets. I'm sure they'll be hungry for something with meat on it right about now."

Mercy tried not to look too closely at the body as she picked up the squirrel by the tail. It was cold, and the fur was soft in her hand. She had never eaten a squirrel before and she felt bad for the creature. Her father would never make her eat squirrel, but then again, he had been a working hunter, not a kidnapper. But she had to play Oscar's games and pretend to be a dutiful daughter. She shuddered to think what would happen if she didn't.

Together they walked to the front yard. She half expected the two werewolves to run at her like Silver had done the other day, but they were both curled up asleep on the ground. Even transformed, werewolves needed sleep apparently. They were far less terrifying asleep, almost cute in their own way, but she was glad to see the metal collars around their necks and the chains still properly attached to them. Oscar was out of his mind, but he still had a sense of self preservation at least.

"Wake up! It's breakfast time!" Oscar shouted. Jamison jumped awake. Silver grunted in annoyance. "Come get your breakfast, boys!"

Mercy glanced between the two of them, and then looked down at the dead squirrel in her hand. Was this some kind of trick? Was Oscar trying to get them to attack her since she was holding a squirrel?

Oscar tossed his squirrel into the grass and then pulled out his blade. The werewolves studied both of them curiously, sniffing at the air. Oscar brought the blade down onto the squirrel in a sickening squelch. He tossed a half to each werewolf. The silver one caught it mid-air, scarfing it down quickly. The other let it hit the ground, approached it slowly, then sniffed at it. He was clearly used to eating more than half of a frozen squirrel for breakfast.

Putting away the blade, Oscar gestured for her to come to him. Mercy wasn't so certain. When he gestured more forcefully, she did what he asked. He met her halfway and quickly grabbed the squirrel from her. "I've got to get this inside before they expect more. The new one is still getting used to his new meal plans here. Don't want to have to lop off limbs already!"

Mercy gaped at him as he limped inside to put the squirrel away, leaving her alone with the two werewolves. She thought back to the way Andrei had respected her when he was fully transformed. It had taken many long nights of being at his side when he transformed. Andrei was vicious at first, but over time grew to trust her. Especially when she brought him scraps in the night. Could these werewolves be tamed in a similar way? Oscar clearly kept them undernourished, which made them weaker. So they would certainly be motivated by food. It would be a useful way to get on their good sides.

The silver werewolf was little more than skin and bones. Seeing him side by side next to Jamison who had been brought with them from Crowsmirth, it was clear just how little Oscar fed them. Just enough to keep them dangerous, and a small enough amount to keep them weaker and more docile. It wasn't too different from the ones at the mill. Except instead of being used up completely, Oscar kept them hanging on by a thread. A different method of torture, but still torture. It felt worse since he probably knew their names too, or at least knew what they were like before he stole away their humanity for the rest of their lives.

Jamison took his time eating his half, crunching limbs and bone awkwardly. He chuffed a few times to get it down. Clearly it wasn't a favorite. But he did sniff the ground after and then looked over at Mercy.

"I'm not your breakfast," she stated forcefully, remembering how she started out working with Andrei's werewolf form. He did seem to understand her and whimpered before looking away. It was a start at least. She would just have to be careful not to let Oscar see her working with them. He would put an end to that real quick.

Oscar returned from the house, drawing all eyes toward him. He no longer had his long blade on him, which made Mercy relax more. The silver werewolf was already bedded down again, but the new werewolf was still hungry. He could probably smell the squirrel and blood on Oscar. He started snarling once Oscar went down the porch steps.

In a flash, Oscar had his gun out and aimed it at him. "Don't you start with me! I'll make you bleed again like yesterday!"

Jamison backed down almost instantly. He looked

between Mercy and Silver as though hoping they would protect him. But that wasn't possible. Nobody could protect him from Oscar.

Despite the threat, Oscar's voice was full of fear. Even though he kept werewolves as pets, he was clearly terrified of them. Interesting. Another observation to file away. As dangerous as it was, shadowing Oscar was giving her more insights into him.

Oscar returned to her side. His hands shook, so it was difficult for him to get his gun holstered again on his hip.

"Damn beasts!" he growled. "Werewolf hunger is never sated, child. Remember that."

That wasn't true. She knew that from her own research on them. But the fact that Oscar believed such nonsense and touted it as truth told her she had more experience with werewolves than he did.

So many pieces of information. So many of Oscar's fears revealed. If only she could find a way to use all of her observations to her advantage.

THE WINDMILL at the power house had seen better days. Oscar had done very little to maintain it, and Mercy grew more concerned as they approached it. The blades turned, but they all squeaked loudly in need of greasing. One had even come a little loose and wobbled as it spun. A couple of them had visible holes in them, which was really bad. One good storm could tear a blade right off, or even tear up a blade so badly the speed would get lowered. If that got low enough, the barricade wouldn't get enough electricity. No electricity, no barricade. The barricade was all that stood between them and the werewolves that clearly still ruled the woods at night.

Oscar could deal with werewolves and kidnapping people, but if he was as terrified of werewolves as he seemed, then he was a fool to put off maintaining the windmill. That had always been the top priority for Mercy and her father. It came before everything else.

They had always kept it in top shape, knowing the dangers should it fail. Mercy had seen the risk firsthand at Kit's home. The windmill and the barricade were as necessary as unspoiled food and clean water. Oscar clearly either didn't know how to fix it or didn't care to. Why in the world would he choose to stay here if he didn't know how to upkeep the grounds? He clearly was disconnected from reality, but an experienced hunter ought to know the dangers of werewolves lurking in the woods.

"Your old man ever let you inside of this place?" Oscar asked, rubbing at his bad leg.

Mercy considered her words carefully. "Sometimes. Not very often though," she lied, not wanting to let on what she knew or what she was capable of. She figured the less information she could give him going forward, the better.

"Sometimes Solomon was a smart man. Not often, but occasionally. I'm sure he didn't want you to get hurt. It's a long fall from the top, and those blades could kill a man if he got too close."

Mercy had to resist the urge to roll her eyes. Of course she knew the dangers. She had been the one to get up there and free the blades on several occasions. Again, he made jabs at her father. Anger flared up briefly, but she pushed it back down. She was getting better at controlling her anger. "Yeah, that's what he said. It was dangerous to go inside."

Oscar settled down on a rock, still rubbing at his leg. "I don't want you to touch any of the equipment of course. That's all too complicated for you to understand. But those stairs aren't so nice to my leg. I don't suppose you would mind cleaning it out some, would you?"

A shudder ran through her at the memory of the spiders she had dealt with every fall back when they properly maintained the power house. She couldn't imagine how bad it had likely become since. Had anyone ever cleaned it?

"Clean it?" she asked.

"Sure. There's a broom inside the door there. You can use that. That won't be so terrible, right?"

Mercy blinked at him. He stored the broom inside the power house that needed constant cleaning? "We used to keep a broom in the shed in the back. I'll go see if I can find it. That'll probably be easier to get than that one will be."

Oscar brandished his pistol and cocked it. "No. You won't. You'll go into the power house and use the perfectly good broom inside there instead. Like a good daughter who doesn't disobey her pa."

Her entire body went rigid as she stared at the gun. She had seen him pull it out on the werewolves, but that didn't dissipate the terror of having it aimed at her. Foolishly, she had believed she had convinced him of her good intentions, but it was clear she wasn't even close.

"You will never enter the shed, especially not without my permission, child. Like the fence and the gate, it is off limits to you."

Mercy couldn't get the spiders out of her mind. "But it's going to be overridden with bugs in there!"

His gaze was icy as he raised his voice. "We have already gone over this! How many more times do we need to repeat the same words? The shed is off limits. Do I make myself clear?"

Mercy flinched. "Yes, Pa."

"Good." He gestured to the power house with his gun. "Now get to work. We're losing daylight and that place hasn't been cleaned in ages. I promise it isn't going to clean itself."

Mercy swallowed down the lump in her throat and went toward the power house, knowing his gun would likely be trained on her the entire time.

THE DOOR CREAKED LOUDLY as she pulled open the heavy door of the power house. Light streamed into the space through cracks between the wood. The power house was built to generate power not be a comfortable place to live, and regularly the insects crawled inside for shelter. As she pushed the door open further, dust fell from above the door frame. Mercy coughed and then her eyes went wide, taking in the sight before her.

Every inch of the space was filled with cobwebs and spiderwebs. There wasn't a patch of wood or a patch of ground she could spot that didn't have one or the other. What she hoped was cobwebs were probably just more spiderwebs. She remembered the spiders liked building webs in the past, but she and her father had never let it get this bad. She leaned out of the doorway, looking for where she used to lean the broom beneath the overhang outside. Of course, it wasn't there. It was inside. Mercy's panic made her desperate to find it and use it as a weapon.

"Where's my broom?" she called back to Oscar, too anxious to turn around and see the pistol aimed at her back.

Oscar chuckled. The sound made the hairs go up on the back of her neck. She was starting to really hate his laugh, especially when he held a dangerous weapon toward her. "Not quite your broom anymore, is it?"

She felt sweat break out on her forehead and closed her eyes in frustration. "No, I guess not, Pa."

"That's right," he said. "Whose broom is it now?"

"Your broom, Pa."

"Good. Should be inside on the left."

Mercy took a deep breath. "Okay," she whispered to herself. She angled her gaze to the side, looking through the darkness and webbing. Patches of sunlight drifted through them as lines across the room, revealing every single spider web that clung within. Far in the corner, ashen from the dust covering the handle and bristles, sat the broom. It too was covered in spiderwebs.

"Doesn't do much good in there," she muttered to herself.

"Hurry up, child. We don't have all day for your dawdling."

"Yes, Pa," she said over her shoulder out of reflex.

Steeling herself, she finally took the plunge. Her hands shook as she used an arm to knock down a web, whimpering at the amount of stickiness that clung to her skin. Her instincts told her to go back and tell Oscar she couldn't do it, but she hadn't survived the werewolves of Crowsmirth just to be squeamish about a bunch of spiders.

She squinted and headed for the broom, trying to keep her breathing calm. Despite waving one arm in front of her, she still felt the webs on her face and in her hair. She was proud of herself for not freaking out, but then she felt something fall on her face that most definitely wasn't a web.

That did it. She dragged her hands over her face, shaking from head to toe, and shrieked as she jumped in place, trying to get all the webs off of her. Outside, Oscar's laughter brought tears as she trembled all over.

She pressed her palms against her eyes and hot tears spilled out. How had it come to this? Of all the things she would have expected to push her over the edge, she never thought a bunch of spiders in the power house would overwhelm her. But tears had been threatening since yesterday. A good cry had been coming, and it never happened at a good time. There was no safe place to cry here. Even when she was alone, she never really felt alone. Tears sprang up no matter how often she pushed them down or wanted a better time to shed them.

Standing in the power house, surrounded by spiders, with spiderwebs and probably spiders in her hair, Mercy cried. She knew Oscar sat outside wielding his gun. And somewhere Andrei, Kit, Thomas, and maybe even Leyda, were looking for her. It all came crashing down. Mercy cried into her hands, tears streaked down her cheeks and soaked her sleeves. After a few moments of tears and sobbing, Mercy looked up at the stairwell that led straight to the top. The blades of the windmill sent shadows throughout the entire structure. Much like the grinders at Farrell Mill, they kept turning despite every-thing. Despite the damage to the blades, the lack of grease, or the rattling at the base, they still turned with the wind, doing what they needed to do. They had to keep going or else the barricade fell. If they stopped turning, people died. If they stopped, this small sanc-tuary would be lost.

It was an odd comfort at a time when Mercy needed it the most.

She took a deep breath, taking in the scent of dust and dirt that told her she was home. That was part of it too, she realized. She hadn't wanted to come back here to the pain that awaited her, or the ghosts that lurked around every corner waiting to jump her. But she couldn't avoid her past forever. She couldn't run from the painful memories of her father, or how she now knew the way she grew up had been abusive. Oscar had forced her back here, but now she understood she had needed to come back all along. This place was a part of her, whether she liked it or not, even with all the bad memories and the good ones. It didn't matter how many werewolves she faced or what chemical compounds she made, this was her home. A part of her would always belong here.

"How's it coming in there?" Oscar called.

She snorted and watched the dust swirl in front of her. She needed to escape this place and stop Oscar from kidnapping anyone else. She needed to focus on more than surviving. She needed a plan. The power house was the only place on the property Oscar couldn't easily reach. It could be a defensible place if she was smart about it. All it needed was a good cleaning. She had spent most of her life cleaning, whether it was her father's home or Farrell Mill. She could do this. She just had to be brave and get it done and out of the way.

With renewed determination, she crossed the rest of the room, shielding her face from spiderwebs, and fetched the broom. She beat it against the wall a few times and coughed at the dust and dirt that floated into the air. Her stomach tightened when she saw all the tiny spiders fleeing from her along the wall, but she refused to flee.

The power house wasn't pretty, but it could be a sanctuary if she took care of it. And she needed some place to call her own, even if it was overrun with spiders.

MERCY WASN'T sure how long she was sweeping and knocking down webs, but by the time she made it to the top, Oscar had left his post at the door. Honestly she had forgotten he was even down there after a while. The realization he had left her to it made her smile. Let him think she was still crying her eyes out. That's probably better for her in the long run anyway.

She considered running for the gate, but the two werewolves were awake. That meant the gate was once again guarded—at least for now. But Oscar's perfect holding cell had cracked here and there. It wasn't as tight of a plan as he wanted her to think it was. Most of it relied upon fear of him, which did work. She gave him that.

Oscar was clearly delusional to think Mercy wouldn't eventually escape from her old home. If she had enough time, she would find a way. Surely he understood that. But his strange desire to be her father clearly was no act. He was risking a lot to keep her here.

Sweeping off the final pile of debris from the opening at the top of the power house, Mercy took a break as a reward to herself. Oscar certainly wasn't going to give her any rewards for getting this place cleaned up. Leaning her back against the archway, she looked out over the woods surrounding the property. The trees had mostly lost their leaves and the dusty road her father used to drive the truck up every day was getting overgrown from disuse, but it was still there. Her eyes misted over at the sight, but she wiped the tears away.

Beyond the house and the shed, close to the fence on

the opposite side of the property, Oscar was collecting from his various traps. He had a satchel with him. She watched as he picked up a large bird, its wings hanging wide when he lifted it into the air.

As the windmill blades beat in front of her in an endless cycle, Mercy realized she could see across the entire property from up here. She could see the full fence line, the gate, the werewolves and their stakes, and the shed. More importantly, she could watch Oscar's path as he checked each trap, pulling out vermin or reaching down to clean off leaves to see if a trap was full. There were more of them than Mercy had realized. He had them all along the fence, ready to catch any small animal that made its way onto the property. It was a smart way to catch small prey.

As Oscar reached down to collect animal after animal, a plan began to form. Mercy narrowed her eyes. It was going to be dangerous—if it even worked at all. If Oscar found out what she was doing, she wouldn't survive. It didn't matter if he wanted her to be the daughter he never had. That would be a final betrayal and he wouldn't let her live.

She rubbed a hand along the frame of the doorway. The power house was more than a place of blessed isolation and a sanctuary in a terrifying way of life. It was a lookout tower. A planning location. It was a way to get her bearings and get a better understanding of her prison when she wasn't stuck on the ground in the midst of it.

After a quick trip to the bottom of the power house and back up again, Mercy stood in front of one of the walls at the top of the power house. She tossed a rock up and down in her hand. She had found a sharp one near where Oscar had been sitting earlier.

She started carving a crude map into the wooden wall: the fence, the house, the shed, and a general estimate on the werewolf ranges. Mostly, she focused on watching Oscar in the distance. Every time he checked a trap, she marked an X on the map.

Mercy smiled to herself as she worked. It felt a little silly right now, but she could see the path ahead. It would take some time, but if it worked, Oscar would regret ever bringing her back home.

PART 2

BLOOD IN THE SNOW

6

JAMISON AND SILVER

AS AUTUMN TURNED COLDER, Mercy played the part of the most well-behaved daughter Oscar could have asked for. She was permitted to go to the power house daily on her own without supervision. As Oscar trusted her more and more, Mercy offered to help cook. He was reluctant to allow it at first, but as the cold bothered his leg more, he eventually relented.

Mercy had to suppress her joy as Oscar removed each of the padlocks on the kitchen cabinets. As the pile of discarded locks grew higher, Mercy knew more freedom on the grounds and her responsibilities began to increase. She had less time to herself during the day, but it didn't matter. Her plan had taken a big leap forward. What appeared to be sympathy and willingness to help out on Mercy's part was really all based on her elaborate plan.

One cold winter evening as snow fell heavy outside, Mercy lay in bed on her side with eyes wide and ears sharp. She had her back turned to the bedroom door, but she fought the urge to sleep. Instead she waited, and she listened to the sounds of the night.

The wind tore through the trees outside, sounding almost like a banshee. The werewolves howled to join it, but Rose's howl always sent a chill down her spine. As the weather got colder, her wolf form seemed more ferocious and dangerous compared to the others. Of the three of them, Mercy feared her the most.

Rose regularly clawed at the front door, probably smelling Mercy and Oscar inside. Every night Mercy listened to her painful screams as she transformed. These soon turned into lonely howls that went on for most of the night. Unlike the other werewolves, Rose was scrappier, more restless. She was always biting at her chain and pacing across the porch, feet thumping an anxious rhythm on the wood. Mercy had no idea why she was more dangerous than the others at night. Was it some effect of the Liquid Lead on the others? Maybe it was because Rose was well-fed compared to the scraps the others got. Mercy had long learned the importance of food to werewolves in their transformed state. The transformation took a lot of energy. Andrei could eat constantly when he was in his human form. Even Jamison and Silver, who didn't transform twice a day, still needed more than half a squirrel to keep them alive.

Footsteps in the kitchen pulled Mercy out of her thoughts. Oscar was doing his nightly ritual of fetching a cup of ale for himself before bed. She heard his distinctive footsteps as he entered the back hallway and came to a stop outside of her bedroom door. This was also a nightly ritual of his, one that made her anxious ever since she first found out about it.

Mercy's bedroom door opened as he peeked inside. The hinges squeaked loudly and he grumbled under his breath. Mercy made a point never to oil those hinges, even though he had asked her to do it a dozen times. No, she wanted to know when he was spying on her.

Mercy didn't move a muscle as she lay in bed. She breathed deeply, eyes wide, and waited. She strained to listen in case he decided to step into the room. He hadn't done it yet, but Mercy wouldn't put it past him. Oscar must have stood there for a solid minute or more before he closed the door and she heard him limping toward his room. She closed her eyes and breathed a sigh of relief. No matter how many times she heard him creep in to check on her, it always made her anxious. It was something a father would do, especially with three transformed werewolves outside, but he wasn't her father.

His footsteps sounded for a few more minutes, then she heard the soft thump of his door closing for the night. She laid there a long time, waiting for more sounds, more evidence he was still awake and moving about. Through the cracks in the shutters, she watched the snow fall dimly lit by the waxing moon in the sky.

Finally when she was certain she hadn't heard him move for a long time, she got to her feet and tiptoed to her door. She got down on all fours and peeked beneath her door toward Oscar's room. Through the dust resettling on the wooden boards, she watched for any sign he could be awake. She searched for any moving candlelight, the creak of a board, or a shadow against the floor of the silent house. She laid there until the floor was warm against her cheek. Still she saw nothing.

Good. That meant he was probably asleep, deep enough he would not hear her movements at least. The fact she didn't know for certain always made her nervous. She had no way of knowing if he was truly asleep or not. Some nights she would lay on the ground watching his bedroom and worry spun like spiderwebs in her mind. Maybe Oscar was laying on the floor staring back at her through the darkness. Maybe he was standing by the door with his shotgun, waiting for her to make a mistake. She shook herself. There was no need to work herself up into a state. She didn't have time to cry in bed again like she had done so many times. She needed to work on her plan if she hoped to get out of this place.

Silently she climbed to her feet and pulled on her thick boots along with a warm blanket. She pulled open the shutters that didn't squeak at all on their hinges. These she oiled regularly, like clockwork. She took one last look back at her bedroom door and climbed outside.

She landed with a crunch as her feet hit the thick, packed snow. Reaching back inside her bedroom, she pulled the shutters closed behind her. Already she was shivering from the bite in the air. It was only December, and she had no idea how cold it would get come February if she was still doing her nightly tasks then.

No, she wouldn't plan that far out. She would be out of this place by then. She refused to allow herself to be caged for that long. She pushed her doubt aside and instead focused on the task at hand.

She unfurled the burlap sack she had found underneath in the kitchen. It was one of several she and her father had used to bring food in from the truck. Normally it was for fruits and vegetables, but these days it carried very different cargo.

Instead of heading to the front gate where the three werewolves lurked, she headed to the shed.

The fairly small building had been built by her father to store tools and werewolf cages. She could spot cracks between the wooden boards, but it was always too dark to see inside. Although the temptation was strong, she refused to try the door. It was covered in padlocks anyway, and she still hadn't worked out how she could get inside. Oscar was a paranoid man, and if she so much as touched the front latch, she felt like he would know. She couldn't risk him finding out about her nightly ventures. If he locked her in her room or boarded up her window, she would truly be trapped. She could imagine him even staking a werewolf outside her window, maybe even Rose. She shuddered. No, she needed to play it safe for now.

She passed by the shed and approached the darkness of the electric fence. Fortunately the snow fell heavily tonight. It would help to cover her tracks.

The hum of the fence told her she was close. As snow fell on top of the fence, there was a soft zapping sound. It was dangerous to be so close to it, especially in the freshly falling snow. Her father used to shovel snow away from it in the dead of winter and make sure each side was clear. More maintenance that simply wasn't done anymore. Mercy slowed her pace until the fence was fully visible, and then she walked the perimeter of the property, keeping a safe distance and watching her step.

It had taken weeks of watching Oscar make his rounds and carving the locations of the traps into the wall of the power house for her to feel comfortable coming out here on her own. The first time she walked the perimeter, one of the traps had gotten too close to the fence and fried the rabbit trapped inside. Another time, she nearly tripped over a cage she hadn't seen for all the debris. A noise that loud might wake Oscar inside, or at least agitate the werewolves. She walked slowly and took her time, determined to be wary and cautious despite the biting cold.

She stopped at the first trap, a cage surrounded by an inch of snow. It was empty. The next one was another cage, rusted on one side, but still strong enough to catch a squirrel or a rabbit. Also empty.

Mercy groaned. The heavy snow was good for covering her tracks, but not so great for capturing prey. Two more traps. Both empty. She was about to give up for the night when she heard a metallic clank up ahead.

She rushed ahead. A flash of white moved inside one of the cages. It was a rabbit! Perfect.

Grinning, she was maybe a foot away when something came up quick beneath her. She jumped back with a yelp. A bear trap emerged from the snow and slammed shut right where she had been standing.

Breathing hard into the cold air, she put a hand to her chest to slow her fast-paced heartbeat.

That one hadn't been on her map. Of course not. If it didn't have anything, Oscar could just avoid it. If that had gotten her, he would know what she had been up to. He would know she had been lurking near the fence. A shudder went through her as adrenaline coursed through her. She took a few deep breaths, trying to slow down her racing heartbeat.

She looked down at the bear trap with inch-long teeth. Instead of snapping her left ankle in two, it had bitten off a corner of her blanket. As much as she didn't want to deal with it, she knew she had to get rid of any evidence she had been out here. Quickly she crouched down in the snow and worked to free the scrap of fabric. The metal was ice against her stiff fingers and tough to open from rust buildup on the bolts for the jaws. Eventually, she pried the trap open and reset it. That was the only way to get the fabric scrap out.

Taking a steadying breath, she got to her feet and stuffed the fabric back into her pocket with freezing fingers. She turned to the rabbit in the cage.

"After all that, I'm really not too keen on killing a rabbit. So you'll have to wait for Pa instead."

The rabbit stared at her with big, terrified eyes and its pink nose twitching. It had moved to the back of the cage, as far away from her as it could get.

Mercy sighed. She really didn't want to leave it for Oscar to find. It was way too cute. It was one thing if they were dead when she found them, but another if they were still alive. She felt bad for anything trapped on the property. Carefully she stepped closer to the cage and opened the door. The rabbit stared at her, frozen with fear.

"Well, go on," she said. "I'm not going to hold this open all night."

Its nose twitched once before the rabbit hurried out of the cage, toward the fence, and escaped through a small hole at the bottom.

Mercy smiled. "So that's how you've been getting in. You're living dangerously, friend." She wrapped her blanket tighter around her. "Though I guess we both are, aren't we?" She reset the trap, fully aware she spent more time talking with wild animals than she did with people. It wasn't so different from when she was growing up here.

Taking her time, she continued around the perimeter, cautious of more sharp teeth hidden in the snow. It was coming down harder now, and it didn't matter how close she pulled the blanket, it didn't stop her from shivering.

Finally she came across three traps, each with a dead squirrel that was frozen solid. She picked them up by the tail and stuffed them into her bag.

Trudging through the snowdrifts on her walk back to the house warmed her up some, and her breath came in little clouds in front of her face. Her fingers were still frozen but at least she wasn't shaking anymore. Heading around the side of the house farthest from Oscar's bedroom overlooking the backyard, she finally made it to the front yard. Stopping at the corner of the house to catch her breath, Mercy realized with frustration that doing this in the winter was far more dangerous than it had been in autumn. She had to wait for heavy snowfall. As the temperatures dropped to colder temperatures, she wasn't sure how she was going to keep this up.

Doing this in the snow took much longer than she had expected. Staring out at the front yard and at the electrified gate in the distance, Mercy could suddenly see the months—maybe years—stretched out before her, trying to bring this plan of hers into action. It had seemed easy back in autumn when she first pieced it all out. All she had to do was deal with fallen leaves then. Now? Now she second guessed herself.

Was this plan of hers even going to work? Was all this hard work even worth it?

Back in autumn, Mercy had made her rounds once a night or maybe once every other night. Now, with the unpredictable snow and freezing temperatures, every-thing was much harder and far more dangerous. She would have to limit herself to once a week, maybe even less frequently. Would it be enough?

Mercy pulled her gaze away from the gate and the freedom it led to and back toward the house.

Three sets of golden eyes studied her. She hitched the burlap sack over her shoulder and headed toward them.

The closest one, the silver werewolf, came out to meet her. His large paws made deep footprints in the snow as he trotted over, clearly excited. When he reached the end of his chain, he sat down, his gaze intent upon her.

"I'm glad to see you're not snarling and barking

anymore," she said as she dropped the bag onto the ground. Mercy had no idea what his name really was, but Rose called him Silver once and she had started referring to him the same way. Rose didn't know his real name and Oscar never gave him any name. It made her sad to know she might never know what he really called himself. Of the two guard werewolves, Silver was the most resigned to his fate. Or at least he had been until Mercy started feeding him regularly.

She leaned down and reached into the bag. "Are you hungry, Silver?"

He opened his mouth wide, almost in a smile. His long tongue lolled out as he panted hot, rank breath into the crisp air.

"Ew, gross!" She waved a hand in front of her nose, but Silver panted harder and started drooling.

She pulled out one of the frozen squirrels. "Ready? Set? Catch!"

Following Mercy's high toss into the air, Silver leaped up and caught the squirrel with ease.

She gaped at him. "We're up to jumping now! I guess you're getting your strength back, aren't you?"

Silver trotted back to his spot near the house beneath an overhang. He dropped the squirrel down on the ground and started munching happily.

The transformation she had seen in him over the last few weeks was astonishing. No longer did he just snarl at her without getting to his feet. He now greeted her and even jumped for food. She had hoped regular feedings would help him regain his strength and energy, but seeing his response made her feel better about her plan already.

If Silver was the only werewolf out here, she probably could have tried to leave already. But there were two others: Jamison, the man who had been captured when Mercy had been kidnapped, and Rose.

Mercy glanced to the front door where Rose stood on all fours, glaring at her. She was the only one of the three without any chemical alteration. She was a werewolf without Liquid Lead or Mercy's partial cure. She was intense and terrifying, not swayed by food or kind words. She looked at Mercy not as a captor bringing food every few nights, but as prey. She didn't want to eat frozen squirrels. She wanted to eat people.

If Mercy wasn't directly involved and putting her life on the line every time, it would have been a fascinating study. Andrei had acted ferociously before he was given her cure, but she hadn't expected this big of a difference between male and female werewolves. But here it was. Evidence as clear as day. If only she had the freedom to study it and understand it. Maybe it was the key to curing the Liquid Lead poison.

A whimper pulled her attention to the newest werewolf of the three: Jamison. Mercy always called him by his name, even if he no longer had his mind. It was only fair since he couldn't talk anymore.

"I'm so sorry, Jamison. I got caught up thinking again. You know me."

She carried the satchel close to him, though careful not to get too close. Unlike Silver's calm patience,

Jamison practically choked himself on his leash, trying to get close to the bag. He drooled so much the fur around his muzzle was covered in ice crystals. He pulled hard on his chain, licking at the air as if Mercy was going to hold up the frozen squirrel for him to lick like a popsicle.

"Hang on a moment." She laughed when he kept licking the air. Finally she pulled out the squirrel and threw it at him. He struggled to catch it in the air. It instead hit him in the chest and fell to the ground a foot or two away from him. It was just far enough away that all he could do was lick at the frozen fur with his long, pink tongue.

Mercy huffed. "Come on, why are you so bad at this? You're a werewolf. You're supposed to be good at eating."

It was funny when this first happened. She thought it was a game for him. But each time Mercy had to toss the squirrel again. She hated having to get so close, especially when he was so hungry.

She moved closer to him, keeping her eyes on him instead of the squirrel. She reached down, felt around in the snow, and grabbed the squirrel by its head. With a grimace, she tossed it behind Jamison. For a brief moment, his sandpaper tongue rolled over the sleeve of her shirt. It was clearly Jamison just being excited, but panic settled in all the same. Jamison turned and ran over to the squirrel, kicking snow on top of her in his wake.

Mercy gave a nervous laugh as she backed away from him, grateful to be out of his range. She looked down at her hands, remembering the bear trap and the cage. If she had any cuts on her hands and he had licked that instead of her sleeve, would she be turned into a werewolf too? She didn't see any fresh cuts on her hands at least, which was amazing considering the amount of physical work she did.

She took a deep breath. It was a stroke of luck and that was dangerous. Trying to calm her nerves, she rubbed her hands on her pants. A chain jingled, and she looked up, expecting to see Jamison coming back for more, but he was still eating and struggling with the fluff on the tail. She glanced at Silver; he had curled up beneath his overhang, trying to go back to sleep.

It was Rose. She stood at the full length of her chain on all fours, completely intent on Mercy. Jamison and Silver might have taken Mercy off of their food list, but she hadn't. Her eyes weren't friendly amber like the others. They were red. When Mercy came around, they were always red.

Without taking her eyes off of Rose, Mercy pulled out the third squirrel.

"Here you go, Rose. A peace offering."

The squirrel fell with a flop at Rose's feet. She didn't even look at it. Instead she revealed her sharp fangs and snarled at Mercy. Jamison and Silver looked over at her before going back to what they were doing. That was an improvement. Before they all used to join in snarling and snapping at her, but now it was just Rose. She was the only one who wasn't swayed by food and frozen meals. But Mercy needed Rose to be on her side if she wanted to use the werewolves to escape. She needed them to be friendly to her, to trust her. Even after a month of full meals, Rose hadn't touched a single one of them and Mercy wasn't any closer to gaining her trust, let alone her help. She sighed. Rose was the only holdout among the werewolves, and she was arguably the one Mercy needed the most.

The cold had started eating through her clothes again, so Mercy gathered her burlap sack, gave one last look to the gate that led to freedom, and headed back to her bedroom window.

Part of her thought she was being a coward. Rose's leash wouldn't reach far enough to the gate to prevent Mercy from leaving. She doubted Silver would give her chase, and Jamison was too distracted by his food to care what Mercy did. Technically, she could get out of the gate and into the woods, but it was a long walk to Kanta at night. The sheer number of werewolves she had seen in Crowsmirth still shook her. Not to mention the many howls that joined in with the three werewolves in their nightly chorus. If even one of them beyond the fence was as intent on tracking down Mercy as Rose, she wouldn't stand a chance, especially on foot without a weapon.

As Mercy neared the corner of the house, a chain clinked again. She turned back to see Jamison wolfing down Rose's squirrel, but Rose stood flush against the house at the full length of her chain, watching Mercy with murder in her eyes. She still had her teeth exposed, a threat and a promise. Behind Rose, the metal bracket that secured her to the wall groaned, and the chain connected to it clinked.

Mercy met Rose's blood red gaze and understood.

As a human, Rose might have given into her fate out of her terror for Oscar. As a werewolf, she plotted her freedom and her revenge on her captors, just like Mercy did. In a way, they had a lot in common and Mercy couldn't help but respect her for it.

Somehow Mercy would have to show her they weren't enemies. They would be stronger if they worked together. If she couldn't convince Rose as a werewolf, maybe she needed to try to prove it to her as a human. Even though Rose barely spoke a word to her, Mercy had to try. She was running out of options.

7

EXPIRATION

MORNING ALWAYS CAME TOO EARLY. It was especially bad after a full evening trudging around in the snow and feeding werewolves in the dead of night. Mercy's body ached. As she slid out of bed, her legs and feet protested. Another downfall of doing her nightly ventures in the winter: it wore her out. But she didn't have the time or the luxury to stay in bed. If she wanted to talk to Rose without Oscar overhearing them, she needed to move quickly.

Her mind was more determined than her body and her head throbbed as she pulled on clothes. She pulled back the shutters a crack, careful not to open it too wide and let in all the cold air. Picking up a spare bed quilt, she stood on her toes to nail it up against the window frame. The quilt hung down in front of the shutters, letting in light but keeping the cold out some. It was a trick she had used as a kid to help keep out the harsh winters.

The snow was still coming down continuously

outside, blanketing the grounds in smooth, white slopes and filling the tree branches. It was quieter than normal out there, save for a single crow cawing into the silence and a strange breathy noise.

She pulled on one of the sweaters that surprisingly still fit her and crept up to the window to peer out through the crack. Jamison stood as close to the corner of the house as he could get and he snorted into the cold air. She could just make out his front half. Powdery snow dusted his shoulders and head. He was less than a dozen feet away from her window and his chain had to be pulled taut for him to be so close. He wasn't close enough to climb inside her window, but he was close enough for Mercy to be uncomfortable.

Jamison shook off the snow and looked around as though he was trying to find a place to get warm. Could transformed werewolves die of hypothermia or get frostbite? She had no clue. Thomas would have probably been able to tell her if she had ever thought to ask him.

Mercy felt sorry for Jamison. She remembered him begging not to be given Liquid Lead that day in the front yard, clutching his quilt and terrified. Mercy hated that she was the one who had dosed him with it. She hated that Oscar made her do it to him, especially when her needles were probably somewhere on the property. It was such a waste. Now, as a werewolf who could never be human again, he might freeze to death, never knowing where he was or why he was here.

Quietly she closed the shutters and replaced the makeshift curtain. She wondered how long the werewolves would last in this weather. Would they make it through the cold winter? She hated how helpless she felt in this place. She finished getting dressed, trying not to think of all the people she couldn't help.

Despite her sweater and thick boots, the air in the house felt brisk since there was no way to keep out the cold completely. Across the hall, Oscar's door was ajar, the room empty. He was always up early, even in the middle of winter, it seemed. She poked her head in just to see if he forgot to lock something away, but as always all the cabinets had padlocks. The bed was fastidiously made. Oscar never seemed to make a mistake when it came to security, much to her annoyance.

She expected to find Rose cleaning up the kitchen like she normally did around this time of morning. Although a stack of dirty dishes sat on the counter, Rose wasn't there. The fireplace blazed in the small living room just beneath her mother's portrait. Mercy looked out the back window, curious to see if she had been roped into helping Oscar outdoors.

"Mercy?"

She turned to see Rose curled up in the armchair. She was covered in so many blankets Mercy hadn't even seen her there. She looked exhausted.

Rose shook her head. "Damn, I must have fallen asleep. He's going to be mad at me." Fear filled her voice as she uncurled herself. Despite the many blankets and the blazing fire right in front of her, she was shivering. That wasn't a good sign.

Mercy stepped in front of her. "No, you don't need to be working right now. You need to rest."

"No!" she cried, gaze darting to the back door. Her

fear of Oscar over her own health was alarming. "I can't rest. He'll beat me if I don't do what he asks." Her teeth started to chatter as she pulled herself to her feet.

Mercy took her hand. Her skin felt clammy. Normally, she would assume Rose was sick, but that wasn't it. In all her time working at the mill, she never saw a single werewolf get sick, even the ones that had been chained to the grinders. No, it was the change. Every night she turned into a beast and every morning she turned back. Even with a werewolf's incredible healing abilities, it eventually wore the body down. Mercy had seen the same thing at the werewolf camp. That was what killed so many of them. The constant demands on the body were too much. Add to that Rose's limited sleep and occasional shocks from Oscar, not to mention the constant physical demands and workload, and it was clear to see where Rose's path was headed. If Rose died on Mercy's watch, it didn't matter that they were under Oscar's thumb. Mercy would never forgive herself. Even worse, she knew Leyda never would either.

"You need to rest." She tugged at Rose's hand.

With tears in her eyes, Rose allowed herself to be pulled back to Mercy's bedroom. "He's going to be so mad at me!"

"Then tell me what needs to get done and I'll do it! Please let me help you."

She looked up as tears rolled down her cheeks. Finally she closed her eyes tightly and sighed before again looking at Mercy. "He wanted me to bake you something for your birthday."

Mercy had expected cleaning the dishes or sweeping out the fireplace, but not that. "What?" she stammered.

"For your birthday!" Rose shrugged. "As if I know the first damn thing about baking anything. That was always Leyda's specialty. Not mine. Everything I ever made burnt to a crisp."

Rose wiped at her cheeks as Mercy continued leading her back to their shared room. Away from the fireplace, she noticed her bedroom was colder. Rose wrapped her arms around herself as Mercy turned down the bed. Helping her under the covers, Mercy tucked her in tight and put an extra blanket on top.

"I'm going to get you a hot drink. But first, I need to know something." Mercy pushed the door to the room closed.

"What do you need? A recipe? Because I'm afraid I can't help you with that."

Mercy shook her head with a bittersweet smile. She wished she and Rose could have gotten to know each other under better circumstances anywhere else but here. She seemed like she might have had a good sense of humor once upon a time before getting infected and before Oscar got his claws dug into her.

"No, not a recipe. I need to know what Oscar did with my things I had on me when he captured me."

Confusion spread across her face, but at least she wasn't shivering anymore.

"I had a satchel on my waist. Injection needles were stored inside. Do you know what he did with them?"

Her eyebrows arched. "Needles?"

Mercy sighed. "Yes, I created a partial cure for werewolves during my time at the mill. If I gave you a dose, it would prevent you from transforming every night. If we don't get you a dose, the transformations will eventually kill you. That's what happens to all untreated werewolves eventually. Turning into the wolf is just too much."

She went still, eyes continuing to search Mercy's.

"Is that—is that what's happening to me? Is that what used to kill off so many at the camp?" Rose's eyes shimmered with tears. This shouldn't have been how she found this out.

Mercy had no idea how many friends Rose had lost over time this way. It wasn't fair to her to find out like this, and she knew that, but they were running out of time. Rose was running out of time.

"I'm sorry. Leyda, Andrei, and I went back to the camp. We administered the cure to whoever was left, but so many had died already. Nobody even knew who we were."

Rose reached a hand out of the blankets and took Mercy's hand tight. "Leyda. She was there? What did she say? I mean, when she found out I wasn't there? Oh no, she must have thought the worst! Does she think I'm dead? Is that it?" Her voice became more shrill as tears took over her words.

Pursing her lips to keep herself steady, Mercy focused on what she needed. "We all thought you were dead. Nobody knew what happened to you, so they assumed you were gone. The pack said they always assumed the worst when people didn't return."

She released Mercy's hand and covered her own

eyes as tears fell. "And I guess soon enough I will be, if what you say is true. Is death from this curse going to be my only escape from this hell?"

"Please, it doesn't have to be. My cure could help! I just need to know where my things are."

She looked up at Mercy with weary, bloodshot eyes. "You expect me to believe that some kid like you created a cure that will keep me from transforming?" She laughed. "Do you even hear yourself? I bet you're barely old enough to drive a car!"

The back door slammed shut. "Rose!"

Icy terror gripped Mercy's heart. "Rose, please. I am trying to help you here, but I need you to believe me. I need you to help me. If I don't get those needles, you will die from this. If you want to live to see Leyda again, I need to know where he put all of it."

"Rose!" Oscar barked. Both Rose and Mercy jumped at the same time.

Rose turned to her with tired, fearful eyes and gripped her hand tight. "Knowing him, he either left it in the truck or he stored it somewhere. Either way, you should be able to find it in the shed. If you can find a way in, that is. He's got that place covered with trip wires and locks. It's the only place I've never been allowed inside. That and the power house." She gave a nervous smile. "But to be honest, I took one look inside of that place and decided never again."

Mercy nodded. She had glimpsed the level of security Oscar kept on the shed from the outside, so she could only imagine what the paranoid man had done inside. But she had to get her cure. It was the only way she could save Rose's life and get to safety.

"I promise I'm going to help you," Mercy said before heading for the door.

Rose shook her head. "I've no idea if you're telling the truth, but you sure are brave, Mercy. Thank you for trying."

———————

MERCY CLOSED the bedroom door behind her, already hearing Oscar's boots stomping around the living room. She winced and braced herself for the rage she would have to face.

It wouldn't be for much longer, she reminded herself. If she could find a way into the shed and find her cure, she could give Rose a dose and save her. They could walk out of this place together. It made her heart swell even thinking about it.

"Rose, if you don't show your hide soon, you'll regret it!" Oscar called, pulling Mercy out of her brief excitement.

Until then, she had to deal with him. She had to face him, even when he bellowed so loud the walls shook. With a deep breath, she headed to the main room. Oscar stood in the living room, staring out one of the windows into the backyard. Did he think Rose had run off? Mercy needed to act quick before Oscar's temper got Rose killed.

"Pa?" she asked in a small voice.

Before she could say anything else, Oscar spun

around. Mercy spotted the gun in his hand only briefly before it fired in her direction. Something loud popped by her ear, making her ears ring. Wood splinters shattered off across her cheek and struck the bridge of her nose. With reflexes that were a little too slow, she cried out and dropped to the ground, covering her head with her arms as she watched him, terrified.

Oscar was red-faced and angry. He was saying something, but all she could hear was the ringing in her ears. He holstered his gun, dragged a hand through his hair, and walked over to her. More words she couldn't make out, though the ringing was starting to dissipate.

Finally realizing she couldn't hear him, he reached down and held out a hand. Mercy looked into his eyes. She was trying to figure out if it was safe or not to take his hand, even as adrenaline kicked in and her hands started shaking. Oscar was clearly disappointed, but he wasn't screaming anymore.

Cautiously she took his warm hand with clammy fingers and he helped her up to her feet. He led her back into the living room and sat her down in the armchair by the fireplace Rose had occupied minutes ago. The seat cushion and blankets were still warm.

Oscar held a finger up and arched his eyebrows. Wait. Okay, she could do that. She nodded.

He went into the kitchen and started rummaging around the cabinets. Slowly Mercy's hearing came back to her as though she was traveling out of a deep tunnel. The crackling of the fireplace was a comfort. Then Oscar slammed a cabinet shut and she jumped.

"Can you hear me now?" he asked, glancing over at her.

"Yeah." She nodded, still feeling numb and jumpy at the same time.

He had almost shot her in the head. A fury filled her along with a tightness in her chest. A few inches over and she would be dead. Sweat broke out on her forehead and her hands trembled in her lap. Oscar was gathering a clean cloth and antiseptic, hardly bothered at all. It was the first time he had ever taken an interest in doctoring wounds he had caused.

Somehow, she found her voice. "You almost shot me." It wasn't an accusation, but a fact.

"Yeah, but I didn't, did I?" He gave her a lopsided smile. She wanted to smack it off his face.

He sat the materials down beside her and looked her face over. "A few nasty cuts I can see, but nothing too terrible." He poured the antiseptic onto the cloth and wiped at her cheek, nose, and around her eyebrow and eyelid. It stung more than she liked.

"Just a few scrapes is all, nothing to worry about." He poured more liquid onto the cloth and Mercy saw several bloodstains on it.

"You could have taken out my eye," she snapped. "Why were you shooting like that?"

Oscar gave her a look before dabbing at her cheek. Mercy pulled her face away from him.

"You could have killed me!" she yelled. Oscar froze for a minute in shock. It was the first time she had raised her voice to him since her first day here. It filled her with a strange mixture of victory and fear. He grabbed hold of her chin, squeezing hard enough to cause pain.

"Be grateful I didn't kill you when you snuck up on me like that, child. With an aim like mine, if I wanted you dead, you'd already have a hole between your eyes."

Mercy glared at him as he dabbed at her wounds, still holding her chin far too hard. Finally he released her and Mercy pulled away from him.

"You're lucky," he said with a warning in his voice. "Looks like you'll heal up just fine."

She glared at him for a long moment before responding with rage in her voice. "Thanks, Pa."

He flinched and turned away from her. The sight of his discomfort emboldened her, and she spat the words out before she even realized it. "My Dad would have never shot at me like that."

Oscar sucked in a breath as though wounded and crawled to his feet. "It's not my fault," he cried. "You were sneaking about while I thought someone had come in and taken you both. Well, they can't have you! You're mine, and I won't let anybody steal you away from me. Not without a fight!"

He paced the room, clomping his heavy boots on the creaky wooden floor and dragging a hand through his hair. Talking about this, she realized he was absolutely terrified. This was what he truly feared, losing the many people he had kidnapped to another more adept kidnapper.

It was kind of pathetic, but still it might be useful to her plan. She would have to be careful though. Even when wound up, Oscar had a very dangerous aim with his gun, something she hadn't truly recognized until now. She guessed he had lots of practice from shooting at the werewolves outside.

He put a hand against the wall, leaning heavily against it and taking the weight off of his bad leg. "I'm sorry, Mercy. This wasn't at all how I planned for your birthday to go. Rose was supposed to be out here baking you a cake, but I have no idea where the hell she disappeared to." He dragged a hand across his face.

Mercy considered lying for her, but the grounds were so small she knew Oscar would find her regardless. So she opted to tell the truth, even if it felt wrong to do so.

"She had to lie down. She said she was exhausted."

That seemed to catch his attention. "Exhausted? I guess she has been here for a bit. She's probably starting to get closer to her expiration." He put his hands on his hips. "Let's see... how long has it been since I caught good ole Rosie? A year? Nine months? Yeah, that sounds about right."

"What do you mean, her expiration?" Mercy didn't like where this was going at all.

"Werewolves get a short life expectancy, child. That's why they're so contagious. Transforming every night eats away at them. Doesn't matter how young or how strong. In the end, it destroys them. I've seen it before."

"What do you mean?" she asked.

"Surely you don't think Rose is the only housekeeper wolf I've kept around? Or that this place has been my only home." He barked a laugh that made the hairs stand up on the back of her neck. "This place has the best protection and is definitely the most isolated, but

I've had four other homes I've used before this one. I've had plenty of housekeepers—men, women, whoever I can find. They all get eaten up by the disease in the end. Usually I try to put them out of their misery before it gets too bad. A kindness, you know."

Mercy felt her heart leap into her threat.

"If she's that tired, it means she's got weeks left. After she's all used up, I'll just capture another." He grinned and Mercy found herself leaning back in her armchair, away from him. "These woods are always full of werewolves, but if there is a dry spell, then there's always Crowsmirth. Wolves there are as plentiful as fish in the sea!"

She couldn't find the words to speak. Not after that confession. Seeing werewolves as having an expiration and putting them out of their misery was the most horrific thinking she had ever heard before. She had to lock her mouth closed to keep from saying something she shouldn't.

Oscar clapped his hands, and Mercy jumped. "Let's not worry about that mess right now. It's your birthday! We should celebrate!" He headed to the kitchen with an excitement Mercy couldn't understand.

"Now I'm not the best baker in the world. Painting is more my forte as you can probably guess, but I'm sure I can come up with something." He started rummaging around in the cabinets. "How old are you again, Mercy?"

She had to unclench her jaw before she could respond. "Fifteen."

Just like that she was expected to forget about her

near death experience and about Rose's expiration and simply enjoy her fifteenth birthday.

Mercy wanted to scream.

OSCAR WASN'T wrong when he said he wasn't a great baker. The cake he made, if it could be called that, had no icing on top and wasn't even fully cooked. So the longer the cake sat on the counter, the more the center fell in. She had taken a bite or two of her slice, but fully intended to get rid of the rest of it when Oscar wasn't looking.

For his part, Oscar hadn't even eaten any of his and instead had drunk through two cups of ale already.

Outside the snow had stopped falling, and the fireplace crackled with warmth. At times it felt like they were in the middle of nowhere, even though she knew that wasn't true. By car, Kanta was a short half-hour drive away. On foot was a different story, especially as cold as it was. Even if she did get Rose a cure from the shed, she knew they couldn't leave the place on foot, not in this weather.

"You know, Mercy, I remember the day you were born like it was yesterday." Oscar was poking at the fire, getting the flames to rise up again around a fresh log.

Mercy blinked at him. The very thought of Oscar somehow being present at her birth filled her with revulsion and a bizarre curiosity.

Oscar settled down into the armchair. "It was snowing hard just like this. Had been for days. I was staying at the old inn in Kanta at the time, doing odd jobs here and there, whatever helped me get by. I think I was doing a bit of signage work for the apothecary back when they had a different owner. I was painting letters on their front door. Exciting stuff for an artist of my skillset, but it paid the bills."

He swirled his cup in his hand.

"The mill was much smaller then with only three grinders, if I remember right. Thomas wouldn't let many people tour the place, so I had to go by word of mouth. But it was way smaller back then. I was out in the cold trying to stay warm while carefully painting letters, freezing my butt off and trying to keep my hand still. Then I heard your father's old rust bucket roll in. He was crying out for Dr. Keene, running for the inn to find him. I didn't give a damn about him, but there was fear in his voice. I knew that. I dropped what I was doing and went to his truck. Anna was there."

He pursed his lips together and had to swallow before continuing on.

"She was standing out there in the snow in nothing more than a thin gown. That's when I knew." He shook his head. "That's when I knew something was very wrong." The flames danced in his eyes as his eyebrows furrowed.

"What was wrong with her?" Mercy asked. Her father refused to tell her anything about her birthday or her mother's death. If it hadn't been for the portrait Oscar had made of her, Mercy might have never known anything about her.

Oscar looked at her distantly, as though he was

somewhere else entirely. "Blood. It was everywhere. It stained the snow, stained the seat of his truck. It covered her legs and her nightgown stuck to her legs." He put a hand to his forehead. "And she looked so damn tired. I had never seen her look so exhausted in my life. She was just standing there having to lean on the truck 'cause she couldn't stand on her own two legs." He pressed his fingers to his eyes and turned away from her.

"Did she die that day?" Mercy asked.

He nodded and gave a heavy sigh. "Shew. It's hard to even talk about it to this day. You would think after fifteen years it would get easier, but it doesn't. It still hurts the same as it did the day I saw her." He shook his head as a frown tugged on his lips. "I think a part of her knew what was going to happen. I think she knew she might die." He wiped at his eyes again, "She told me that whatever happened to her that I shouldn't let anything happen to you. That I ought to take care of you and Solomon."

He gave a bitter laugh and knocked back the rest of his ale.

"I wonder sometimes if she was delirious. The fact that she thought Solomon wanted me anywhere near him or his precious daughter is ridiculous." He pursed his lips together and gave her a sad smile. "I'll take a wild guess and say that blowing her child's head off was the exact opposite of keeping you safe. Let alone kidnapping her." He sucked on his lip as he dropped his cup onto the side table.

"Why are you keeping me here? If she wanted you to keep me safe, what is all this for?" He glanced at her and back at the fire, so she pushed again. "Why can't you just let me go?"

He folded his arms and studied her. "The last time I saw you, you were nearly killed by a swarm of werewolves in Crowsmirth. You were wearing rags around your face and pretending to be a hunter. Amid dozens of professional hunters. You're lucky none of them saw through your disguise like I did."

"I had friends with me. We were getting by without your help."

"Oh, were you? Running down the stairs from werewolves was a safe idea to you?"

"If you hadn't drawn them inside with a corpse, I think we would have been perfectly fine!"

He shook his head. "That doesn't count. Regardless of the details, you weren't safe at all. And spending time around Thomas Farrell? He's the definition of dangerous. Have you seen how he keeps his werewolves? You may think I'm a monster, but he's way more cruel if you ask me. No, here you're safe. Here I can make sure you stay safe."

Mercy shook her head in disbelief. "You nearly shot my head off for my birthday. You really think staying with you is safer than me having the freedom to do what I want?"

He pushed himself up to his feet and started pacing back and forth in the small space between the dining table and the fireplace. "Like I said earlier. That was an accident! A slip up, is all! Quit making such a big deal out of it."

He balled up and uncurled his fists over and over

again. He could barely contain himself. But she had to try to understand his twisted motives. What if next time it wasn't just an accident? What if the next time his temper got her killed?

"My Dad tried to keep me safe here too, and now he's dead. Why do you think you'll do any better? Why can't you just give me back my freedom?"

He picked up his wooden cup from the side table and hurled into the fire. Mercy jumped back. The cup caught flame with a whoosh and filled the room with an acrid smell. "I am so damn tired of hearing about Solomon Pinkerton! If he hadn't been so slow to act, so dim-witted to know she was struggling, maybe Anna would be alive today!"

He approached Mercy in several quick steps, looming over her. His breath smelled sour, and she curled her nose against it.

"You know what? Maybe he would be alive too. Maybe if he was so smart, he wouldn't have been shot dead by hunters and devoured by werewolves in the woods!"

Mercy was too stunned to speak.

"I don't want to hear you talk about him ever again, you hear me? I don't want that man's name to be uttered in my home. No daughter of mine should even speak of that murderer's name again. Do I make myself clear?"

She wanted to point out his hypocrisy. That his home was the house her father had built. That for all his talk of being brave and clever, he was holed up here being terrified of the werewolves he kept. That he was so determined he would keep her safe that he nearly shot her. Mercy wanted to slap him for talking so poorly of her parents too, but then her gaze drifted to the loaded gun on his hip and she pushed back all the retorts.

"Yes, Pa. Whatever you say."

"Good. Excellent." He dragged a hand through his thinning black hair and stared for a moment out the back window. "I need to go check the traps. They've been emptier than normal. I'm thinking about putting out traps for those damn crows I keep seeing nosing about." He went to the back door and pushed it open, letting a freezing breeze sweep into the house, before he turned back to her. "With Rose out of commission, I'm going to need you to pick up the cleaning and the cooking around here. Think you can handle that?"

Mercy almost reminded him she had been cleaning and cooking already, but decided against it. As much as she hated holding her tongue, she had to think of survival and escape more than her pride.

"Sure, Pa. No problem."

"Great." He stepped out, his feet crunching on the snow, then he turned to her. "Oh, and happy birthday, Mercy."

The door slammed shut behind him. Mercy looked around at the spilled ale near the fireplace, the flopped cake on the counter, and her own abandoned slice of birthday cake. She still had to make a warm drink to bring to Rose.

She sighed. "Happy birthday to me, I guess."

8

A LITTLE SNOW

THE ICY WIND **FROZE** Mercy's face and made her nose run as she sat beside her bedroom window. It got dark so early now as the winter weather drew in closer. She pulled the blanket close around her shoulders. Stars filled the clear sky and the full moon made the fallen snow gleam as night fell. In the distance, some crows were still cawing. Oscar hadn't been able to catch any of them and Mercy was glad about it.

Rose screamed in the distance. Her transformation got more and more painful every night, but it sounded especially bad tonight. She wondered how long they had been getting worse and she simply hadn't noticed. Was it for several weeks? Maybe even a month? She should have been paying attention to the patterns. She should have seen Rose's decline earlier. If she had, she would have acted sooner. It shouldn't have gotten to the point of Rose's exhaustion and having to sleep almost all day long. Mercy had been so focused on her complicated plan and on escaping she had forgotten she wasn't the only person trapped here. Rose was kidnapped, as were Silver and Jamison. They were all victims of Oscar's cruelty.

As a scientist who had worked so closely with and studied werewolves, Mercy admonished herself for not taking note of the changes. She should have been aware of Rose's struggles long before it came to this. But Oscar was distracting her. He had a way of crawling under her skin and sparking her rage more than anyone she had ever met. Perhaps it was his lack of empathy, his joy in his cruelty, or maybe it was the lack of logic to his actions. Oscar drew her attention away from people who truly needed her. Add that to the long list of reasons she hated him.

The front door slammed shut as Oscar came back inside. Mercy pushed her shutters closed and dropped the hanging quilt back into place in front of it. She crawled onto her bed and stretched out as she heard Oscar's limping footsteps move through the house. She could almost count the seconds it took him to remove his boots, remove his jacket, and make his way toward her. She picked up the mug of hot tea she had made for herself just as the doorknob to her bedroom started to turn.

Right on time, Oscar stepped in. His face was red from the cold outside and he sounded a little breathless. He glanced from her to the mug she cradled in her hands. "You heading to bed soon?" He looked offended, as if he had set some unknown curfew and she was expected to follow it.

"After I finish this tea, I will," she said, gesturing to the warm mug in her hands.

He nodded. "Good. You ought to be in bed already. It's only going to get more busy with Rose out of commission completely now. I'll need your help more around the house to help keep this place running. So make sure you're ready to get up early."

"Rose was louder tonight. Is that normal?" Mercy wanted to know how much time she had left. She wanted to know what stages she needed to look toward moving forward, but pulling information out of Oscar was a delicate and careful process. She had to be careful not to be too curious around him or else it could raise suspicion.

His gaze went distant as he wiped his mouth with the back of his hand. "The disease tears their bodies apart over time. The wolf gets stronger every night while the human gets weaker until the body can't contain them both anymore. The wolf always wins out in the end, but the human body wilts away. Eventually they always die. It's not a bloodbath, if that's what you're worried about. It's more of a crumbling whimper."

Mercy pursed her lips. She hadn't noticed Andrei's werewolf form getting stronger over time, and she would have noticed. She took copious notes on him every night. Was this Oscar's unbiased observations, or was his fear of Rose's wolf form growing with each passing night? Mercy remembered how Rose had pulled at the bracket that chained her to the wall. Maybe Oscar had reason to fear. Regardless of how exhausted Rose was during the day, her wolf form clearly had plans of escape and revenge.

"It was pretty loud tonight, but I guess I might have heard wrong. They all get loud once they start howling," Mercy said.

"Rose is a fierce one, I'll give her that. But don't you worry your little head about her. She won't live long enough to hurt you or me."

Mercy's eyes went wide as her hands shook. The hot tea sloshed in her mug. She was trying to find out information, not get him focused in on killing Rose. She swallowed down her nerves and gave what she hoped was an agreeable nod.

Oscar gripped hold of the edge of the door. "Get some sleep, Mercy. I'll need your help first thing tomorrow."

"Yes, Pa," she said on reflex.

He closed the door and she listened while his heavy footsteps retreated across the hall and into his room. Shortly after, his bedroom door closed with a click. She waited several minutes before returning to her spot by the window. She pulled back the quilt and pulled back the shutters with ease. The blast of icy air made her eyes water. She blinked the tears away as she sipped on her hot herbal tea.

Across from her window sat the shed. When Mercy was younger, she thought it was an eyesore, but now she was grateful. Staring at it helped her come up with a plan. Each night, she looked out, and the shed stood there waiting for her. Each night, she tried to figure out how to get inside.

What she really wanted to do was climb out and test the locks up close, but the perfect bed of fallen snow meant she would leave footprints behind. Even if she tried to cover her tracks, Oscar would notice. He would notice something sizeable moving across the snow and possibly even pinpoint it as human. There would be no way to hide her tracks that wouldn't lead straight to her window. If he didn't take his rage out on her, he would choose one of the werewolves. Based on his current obsession and fear, that might possibly spell the end for Rose.

She sipped the hot drink, the liquid warming her throat and stomach. She sipped, and she plotted. As much as she would like to, she couldn't risk writing anything down in her shared bedroom, not like she had in the power house. Sharing a space with Rose and Oscar monitoring her every move, she simply couldn't chance it. So everything had to be kept inside her head, bottled up and spinning endlessly with her growing fury and worry.

Not too far from her window, a werewolf howled, and the others joined in. The loud, lonesome sound made her heart speed up. She had grown to respect the sound that rattled her entire body every night. In its own way, it was beautiful and completely reflected her own feelings about this place. She longed for freedom, just like they did. But it could also be one of the last sounds Rose made, and that knowledge made her grit her teeth.

"Hold on, Rose," she whispered as the wind howled through the pines and bare oaks. "I'm going to get both of us out of here. I don't know how, but it's going to happen. Just hold on to your human form a little longer." She stared up at the starry sky above. "All I need is a little snow to cover my tracks. Come on, clouds. Give this to me. To us. We need it."

TOO MANY DAYS PASSED, almost an entire week. The sky remained clear and the clouds only occasionally flitted by. No new snow fell during the evening or even during the day. Every night Oscar took Rose outside to chain her up for the night Mercy feared it would be her last transformation. Rose looked worse every day, spending almost the entire time in bed. She could at least get dressed at dawn each day and came inside to wake up Mercy and climb in her warm bed. Mercy knew eventually she wouldn't be able to pick herself up out of the snow. She wouldn't be able to withstand the blood loss she suffered every night and every morning. She didn't think Oscar would let her live long once she became that much of a burden to him.

After days of handling chores from sun up to sun down, Mercy was drained, exhausted, and almost ready to give up on her elaborate plan. The more obstacles she met, the more she worried they wouldn't make it. If Rose died, Mercy wasn't sure if she would be able to face Leyda's grief a second time.

Late one night, as Mercy sat at her window for her nightly vigil of the shed after listening to Oscar go to bed a long while ago, a light dusting of snow began to fall. She stared up at it, mouth dropping in awe. The clouds had rolled in swiftly that night, but she hadn't dared to hope. Yet here it came. But a light snowfall wasn't nearly enough. She could barely see it against the trees in the distance. Knowing her luck, it would soon stop and she would be back in this frustrating waiting game. Then the snow came down heavier. Soon, the partially frozen remnants of snow and mud on the ground were covered with a thick layer of fresh, powdery snow. It was coming down hard.

Mercy stared up at the sky in pure joy. Her breath came in cloudy puffs as more and more snow fell. It wasn't just a heavy snowfall. As the wind picked up and howled through the trees, she realized it was turning into a blizzard.

Moving quietly, she pulled on her warmest coat and heavy boots and crawled out of her window. The wind beat against the house and tried to take her breath away. She had asked for a little snow. Instead she got this. Though thankful, she was also a little scared as she stepped out into it and could barely see a few feet in front of her in all directions. She pulled her blanket tighter, focused only on the shed ahead of her. She could have checked the traps, fed the werewolves to make sure they still trusted her like before, but she refused to entertain any other ideas. They had limited time. She needed to save Rose's life. That meant entering the only place on the property she had no idea how to get inside. The one place Oscar had completely forbid any of them to go.

Back when Mercy used to live here, the shed had several windows. They always closed the shutters tight on them in the winter and put up warm blankets to tuck into the cracks and crevices to keep the cold out. As much as she and her father stored in the small building, they needed lots of daylight to see everything in there.

Oscar had different plans. Every window she used to take careful pains to keep shuttered and wind proofed in the winter had been boarded up. It was a sloppy job, too, judging by the rusty nails that poked out of the boards. He could have at least had the decency to hammer the nails in the right way. Though remembering how she had to do most of the work when they boarded up the front door at the inn in Crowsmirth, she wasn't that surprised. For a man who kept people on hand to do his dirty work all the time, he didn't know how to maintain or repair any of his equipment on his own.

Boarding up the windows was a strange choice. The only conclusion she could make was Oscar didn't want anyone looking inside. Or rather, he didn't want Mercy or Rose to look inside. The pickup truck he owned had to be in there because she hadn't seen it anywhere else on the property. What else did he keep in there that he was so afraid of them finding?

Slowly she circled the building, looking for any way in. The wind and snow seeped into the seams of her clothes and froze her skin, but Mercy wasn't dressed in a mere blanket this time. She was ready for it. She tightened her coat around herself and trudged on. The door to the shed had about a half dozen padlocks on it. True paranoid Oscar fashion. That meant using the front door was out of the question.

What was truly odd were the many metal chains that hung down from the roof. In the wind they clanged against the wooden boards, making a racket. They surrounded the entire building, disappearing into the walls at the top so she had no idea what they were attached to. The smarter move would be to fall back and try to figure out the chains by watching Oscar work with them. But he had keys to the front door, and she had watched him for days going in and out of the place. He didn't touch the chains.

She considered trying to steal his keyring but sighed hot breath into the brisk air. That could take months to find, let alone figuring out which key fit which lock. Knowing how many padlocks he kept around the house that would be practically an impossible task. She didn't have weeks, let alone months. For all she knew, this could be her only chance to find a way inside.

On the wall of the shed, Mercy found a board used to cover one of the windows that she had suspected might be loose. When she tugged at it, the wood gave easily. All she had to do was pull out a nail or two and she could get in. Perfect!

Mercy squatted down to start the task. She got one nail partially out, but one of the chains kept getting in her face. The cold metal brushed against her nose and sent a chill down her already cold spine. At one point, it pinched her cheek, and she pulled away from it. Finally, with a growl, she pushed the chain aside, surprised to feel it had some slight resistance.

The loudest whistle she had ever heard pierced the empty night air. Mercy's stomach dropped, and she cried out in surprise. She looked up to where the chain hung down from the wall, but she couldn't see anything that would be making that much noise. It had to be something hidden inside the shed.

"We've got an intruder!" Oscar screamed from inside the house. "Mercy, hide! We've got a prowler afoot."

With a whimper, Mercy climbed to her feet, intent on running back to her room and climbing in through the window. Instead she froze.

Despite the snow coming down as heavy as it was, her footprints would clearly lead from her bedroom window to the shed.

Images sprang to mind of Oscar boarding up her bedroom window or locking her inside her room every night. Seeing how he cared for his captured werewolves, he could easily keep her here for years. All the work she had made to gain his trust would be dashed in a single night. She would lose access to the kitchen and maybe even the power house. She couldn't let that happen. Not for herself and not for Rose.

No, if Oscar wanted an intruder, she would give him one.

She ran to her bedroom window, then back out to the shed, making the tracks as messy as possible and counting down the seconds she had left.

Oscar would grab his boots, his gun, and maybe even his coat due to the blizzard. That took him several seconds to accomplish, especially with his limp.

Next, she ran around the shed forwards and backwards three times in total. If he was smart, he would take the back door out. But he might be too startled and hurried to think clearly. That would mean —

A werewolf snarled and Oscar screamed. Mercy smiled. She would have to thank Rose later.

"Damn you, Rose!" Oscar screamed, and the front door slammed so hard snow fell like dust from the roof.

The back door would be his next goal. Mercy took off to the fence line, taking deep, shuffling steps as she ran. She hoped the footprints she left looked as big, messy, and clumsy as she felt making them.

With the overcast sky and blizzard, it was hard to see the electric fence up ahead. Mercy held her breath for the last two steps until she heard the electric hum over the howling wind. Her eyes adjusted enough to see the outline of the fence.

"Okay, where to next?" she whispered to herself.

Above her head, long branches reached out, leaving a few bare patches of earth where snow hadn't landed. The fresh snowfall hadn't reached this spot, not yet at least. She stepped on a bare patch of earth, one arm out so she didn't touch the electric fence.

Oscar busted open the backdoor of the house. He was carrying a rifle Mercy hadn't seen before. Did he keep all of his firearms in his bedroom? She hadn't seen them anywhere when she checked it several times, but he must keep them in his closet to have such a big weapon hidden so well. He rushed for the shed, slowing down in the heavy snowdrifts, and Mercy picked up the pace. She scoured the ground for bear traps or anything else as she made her way around the property. She was opposite the back door when one of the werewolves howled. She looked back over her shoulder. The shed was barely visible. Inside, a light flickered through the cracks of the boarded-up windows as though candles had been lit.

For once, Mercy was grateful for Oscar's paranoia. He was too worried about his shed to worry about checking the fence line. As she took another step, her back leg wobbled, and she accidentally kicked one of the trapper cages. She glanced down in horror to see a gray, fluffy tail almost covered in snow. Its motionless hind leg stuck out between the bars of the cage. It looked like a squirrel had been there for several days. With so much to do around the house and the limited daylight, Oscar hadn't been checking the traps as much.

She glanced back to the shed, but she saw no movement there or near the fence. The wind howled and shook the trees above her head, making big glops of snow fall down on her. She hoped it would cover her at least partway.

Taking the long way around the backyard, Mercy ran for the back door. She put her hand on the doorknob, turned it, and froze.

Another idea came to mind. She knocked some of the snow off her shoulders, then opened and slammed the back door shut.

Opening up her coat some at the top, she purposefully shuffled her feet as she went around the edge of the house near Oscar's bedroom window, the side of the house, and finally to her window. Then she shuffled along the same path she had taken before, toward the shed, obscuring her old tracks with new ones.

Her heart pounded in her chest as she heard Oscar continuing to move things around in the shed. Was he afraid something had been stolen? He couldn't know the value of Mercy's needles. Other than his old beat up truck and his numerous captives, what else did he have of value? Surely he didn't have a store of money in there.

Once she was certain she had shuffled her feet enough to make a mess of the tracks from earlier, she decided to speak up.

"Pa, is everything alright? What was that noise?" Her heart thundered in her chest as a silence fell upon the shed before heavy footsteps moved toward the door.

Oscar pulled open the shed door, pouring candlelight out onto the blanket of snow. "Mercy? What the hell are you doing out here?"

"I heard a loud noise!" Her voice wavered out of fear that wasn't difficult to muster to the surface. "What happened?"

He put a hand to his face, making flustered sounds. "I don't care what you heard. I said hide, damn it! Now get inside and take cover. This prowler could be hiding anywhere." His gaze drifted to the front of the house. Mercy spotted both Rose and Jamison watching them, their eyes glinting with excitement through the curtain of snow. Jamison's glowed amber, but Rose's eyes glowed red.

"Damn them. What's the point of having guard werewolves if they don't even chase down intruders?"

Before Mercy could answer, he pointed a finger at her.

"Get back in that house before I lock you in there!"

"Yes, Pa!" She turned and moved quickly toward the house.

"Get to your room and close it up tight! I don't want to see hide nor hair of you until morning."

"Yes, Pa!" she called over her shoulder, careful to show him how she took the same path as before, back to the house and to the back door.

Once closed inside her room, Mercy kicked off her wet boots and long-sleeved clothes, pulled up her blanket, and crawled into bed. She lay there under the covers as blood circulated back into her fingers and toes. Cold, damp hair stuck to her forehead as she took deep, steadying breaths. Her heart was finally slowing down to its normal pace. She dropped a hand onto her chest, feeling the thud against her fingers. She was smiling, grateful to have gotten out of that mess. But she pushed the elation aside.

"That was way too close," she whispered to herself. "Next time, plan first, Mercy. Let's never cut it that close again." She chuckled softly. "I don't think you can be that lucky twice."

It felt a little strange talking to herself, but it wasn't that different from talking to rabbits and werewolves, was it? Honestly, she was kind of proud of herself for thinking so well on her feet, even if she did feel like collapsing for a few days from the stress of it all. Now she knew how Oscar kept his shed safe because locks just weren't good enough for him. The man had to have chains everywhere attached to whistles. If he had caught her out there, there would be no smiles. She shuddered.

She closed her eyes and listened to the snow hitting the wooden walls of the house and the occasional footsteps of the werewolves in the snow outside. Oscar was right, the werewolves should have at least started howling or snarling to alert him there was an intruder. But Mercy wasn't an intruder. She was a friend who fed them. At least most of them. Even Rose was used to her moving around the property, so they hadn't been alarmed when she set off the whistles. Not like they probably would have for a real intruder.

She took a deep breath and felt her eyelids start to close. Maybe her plan for befriending the werewolves was more helpful than she expected it to be.

9

PROMISES

MERCY STOOD BEFORE her window only dressed in thin pajamas, but it wasn't cold. She felt the cracks in the bare wood beneath her feet and her thin cotton clothes fluttered against her skin from the persistent wind. Outside, it was night and stars sparkled in the sky. A golden light spilled out onto the snow from behind her as though the fireplace was at her back, throwing her long shadow against the snow. There was a beauty to it, but also a very clear danger too.

She had been staring at the stars when she heard a footstep in the snow, a light step almost like it was made from a house cat. She looked at the snow again to see her father standing in snow so deep she couldn't see his shoes.

Dad's stubble had gotten long and his eyes were red. Had he been crying? His bloody hand hung at his side, dripping crimson onto the powdery white snow at his feet.

She remembered the dream she had of him before,

telling her to be brave. Did he not think she was brave enough? Was that why he came to her like this? Did he not think she was trying hard enough?

Mercy told him everything that had happened with detailed gestures. Her father heard none of it because no sound would come out of her mouth. She stomped on the ground in frustration. Behind him, the acts of her life she tried so vehemently to convey to him were acted out as if on a stage with performers. But he wouldn't turn to look at them.

She watched as phantom-Mercy slid out of her bedroom window, circled the shed, and accidentally pulled a chain and sounded the terribly loud alarm that hurt her ears. She pointed as Oscar came outside with his rifle in hand. But her father wouldn't turn. He only stared at her with sad eyes.

"Turn around!" she cried, but the sound couldn't leave her mouth.

Her father stepped closer to her window, his footsteps impossibly quiet. He lifted his arm and placed his bloody hand on the window frame. The blood slipped down the window ledge and pooled at her feet. Soon she stood in a puddle of it. The warm sticky sensation was under her toes, but she couldn't move her legs to back away. This was her father and he needed her.

In an instant, the frustration she felt no longer mattered. The reenactments behind him ended. All she could focus on was his face and the deep pain she saw there etched forever into the cracks around his frown and the weariness in his eyes. His parched lips opened, and he spoke words that thundered in her mind despite their frailty.

"He is going to kill you."

Mercy knew who he was talking about: Oscar. She shook her head. She couldn't believe that, couldn't even entertain it. "No," she said through soundless lips.

"You are running out of time. You must be brave, sweetheart." Tears filled his eyes. "You have to act, even if it's difficult. Don't let fear stop you." He reached out and took her hand in his undamaged one. His skin was icy, but she would recognize the texture of his touch anywhere. "This is not the time to hold back." White spittle formed at the corner of his mouth. "Promise me, sweetheart."

"I promise," she whispered, finally hearing her own voice again, though it was warbled and weak.

He reached his bloody hand out and touched her cheek. "I love you."

A shiver tore through her at the coldness of his touch against her face. "I love you too, Dad."

Her eyelids fluttered open as the words escaped her lips with a sigh.

Mercy stared at the ceiling of her bedroom, bundled beneath the blanket and sheets along with the clothes from last night. Closing her eyes, she tried to bring back her father's face, but already the haze of dreaming made it difficult to remember accurately. What shook her the most was how real it all felt. The feel of his touch, the blood on the ground, even the heat of the fire behind her.

She knew she could have reached out and felt her

father's stubble. Each individual whisker would have pricked her fingertips. She wished she had said more to him, done more than stood there in shock and yelled at him to turn around. Why did she never say what she really wanted to say in her dreams? Her eyes misted over as she stared up at the ceiling.

As hazy as the dream already felt, there was one truth she couldn't deny. Her father was terrified for her.

Mercy had to admit last night was scary. If Oscar had even suspected she had gone to the shed, she might be dead along with her parents now. He was that unpredictable and that quick to rage. She knew if he found out, it wouldn't be locking her up. That level of betrayal would mean her death. She knew that now.

Her father told her she needed to be brave. She needed to act. But how could she do that if the entire shed was rigged with those loud whistles? Of course, there was also the nagging question that plagued her ever since she woke up.

What if it was only a dream?

Mercy had certainly been in enough terrifying situations already to prompt the worst nightmares. Maybe it was only her unconscious mind expressing all her fears as she slept. As a scientist, that was the most fact-based answer, even if it didn't feel right. She couldn't trust her feelings on important matters any longer. Not after trusting Oscar and having him drug and kidnap her. To trust her feelings alone could lead her to getting hurt again and again. No, it simply wasn't logical, let alone smart. She couldn't let a bad dream dictate her actions. The shed would be there. She still had time to play it smart and take her time examining it before trying again.

With a groan, Mercy flung her legs over the edge of the bed. Her bare feet landed on the cold wood and she shivered as she sat up.

A cold liquid slid down her cheek. Probably just melted snow from the night before, she mused. Her hair had been pretty wet from being outside. She wiped at it and glanced down to her fingers to see bright crimson.

Her eyes went wide as she wiped at her cheek with her other hand. More blood. She crept to her wash basin and cracked the thin film of ice on top of the bowl of water. She scrubbed at her face and hands.

That wasn't her blood, she realized with a gasp. That was where her father had touched her cheek—with the hand that had been shot shortly before his death. Marking her, or warning her?

Maybe she needed to heed her father's orders. He was trying to tell her not to delay. She had to try the shed again.

It hadn't merely been a dream; she realized with a sinking feeling. Her father really was trying to warn her she was running out of time. No more complicated plans. The next time she saw a chance, she would take it. She had no choice. Otherwise, Oscar was going to kill her.

She swallowed down the fear at that thought. "I won't let you down, Dad," she whispered as the first rays of dawn crept in through the shutters. "I promise."

THE BLIZZARD CONTINUED ALL DAY, much to Mercy's annoyance. She could only hope it came down so hard tonight when she would need the cover and not wear itself out during the day.

She wasn't the only one annoyed. Oscar grumbled about it all day in between drinking mugs of heated ale. The snow made it impossible to chase down the intruder from last night, much to her relief. But it also meant Oscar was cooped up in the house with Mercy and Rose all day. Mercy hoped he would go out to the shed to work or go out and chop some more firewood, since they were getting low. Then she might get alone time with Rose and tell her more about the cure she wanted to give her. But Oscar was too paranoid today. In fact, he hovered around more often than usual.

It was early evening, and the blizzard was as heavy as ever outside with whiteout conditions. Mercy had already had to cook breakfast and lunch, change all the linens, wash all the dishes, can vegetables, and she was tired. She hated how the amount of work she did now made her exhausted in the evenings, when she needed her energy the most. Part of her suspected that was Oscar's plan, but she had no proof of that yet. So far, it seemed like he did the same to everyone he allowed to work inside the house. He worked them to the bone.

Mercy was stuck making soup, a common meal, since the cold seeped into the house and they all suffered from the constant chill despite the blazing fire. She wiped at her brow with the back of her hand as she pulled the pot of soup out away from the fireplace with the fireplace poker. Then she stirred in a big bowl of butternut squash with a large wooden spoon.

Oscar paced behind her. His heavy boots clomped across the floorboards, reverberated beneath her feet, and made Mercy a nervous wreck. He had been pacing off and on all day, watching her work and giving her pointers about how she was doing it wrong. It was getting on her last nerve and she needed to keep him thinking she was on his side for as long as possible.

"Is that the last squirrel we've got?" he asked, gesturing to the pot of soup Mercy tended.

"Last few scraps left," Mercy said, glancing at him. "You could go see if you could hunt a few. It would definitely make the soup richer."

He barked a laugh. He had been drinking consistently since morning and Mercy noted the way he was a little off-balance on his feet. Maybe he might shoot himself in the process and rid her of the trouble. She could only hope.

"I'm far too drunk. My aim would be terrible. And those rodents are far too quick." He went to his barrel and got himself another cup. At this rate, Mercy was worried about what he would do if he got too drunk. Maybe she would get lucky and he would just fall asleep. However, he was hardly known for his cool and calm demeanor when sober. She doubted he would magically get better when drunk.

Mercy glanced at the armchair where Rose sat, or rather, where she was curled up. Despite the blazing fireplace and a couple of blankets, she still looked cold. Her skin had an unusual ashen tint and Mercy noticed that she clearly had trouble dressing after her change overnight. Her dress was on backward and, even though she had some ruffles near her throat that had to be driving her mad, she hadn't tried to change it or asked for help. Mercy kept thinking of her father's warnings. She was running out of time and Oscar was going to kill her.

If Rose was having trouble dressing herself after the change, then it wasn't long before she wouldn't be able to do anything afterward. Her expiration, as Oscar so callously called it, was coming along quickly.

Perhaps if the blizzard had them all locked up together with food running out, that was what would make Oscar lose it. She could see it happen. The man's temper was dangerous. He always kept a loaded weapon on him regardless of how much he drank too. The more she thought about it, the more she wanted to get him out of the house and sobered up. She just had to think of something for him to do that wasn't here with them.

"What about the traps?" Mercy asked.

"The what?" Oscar asked as he spilled some ale on his chest.

"The traps around the perimeter. You know, the ones you showed me that catch small animals like squirrels and rabbits. We could use those. You know, before the crows get to all of them."

"Oh yeah," he said, completely not interested. "Too cold." He waved her off.

She sighed. Running out of time. Need to be brave. Her father's words circled in her mind like a mantra. "Maybe the intruder wasn't a person but a predator looking for an easy meal. If there are a bunch of full traps, it could lure them inside the perimeter. We don't want that to happen."

Mercy wiped her brow again and turned around to see Oscar only a foot behind her, staring at her. Her stomach tied up in knots, but she forced her face not to betray her surprise.

"I'd check them myself," she said with a forced smile. "But you said you don't want me near the fence without you there, right? You would have to come with me, if you want me to check them."

Oscar stared at her with a seriousness that was frightening. "Is that your theory for last night? A predator?" His eyes shone in the firelight at her back. It was oddly similar to the firelight she had seen in her dream with her father. She swallowed down the dryness in her throat.

Her hands felt too warm from being so close to the flames, but she didn't back down from his intimidation. If this was some kind of test and he suspected her of something last night, then he would have to try harder to get the truth out of her.

"A predator, that's what I said." She crossed her arms. "I mean, we're just spit-balling ideas at this point though, right? I mean, you said you didn't see anything out there."

Oscar blinked and averted his gaze. Maybe it was more drink talking than intimidation, but either way, she didn't like it. Oscar gave her the creeps on a good day, but now he gave her gooseflesh in front of a roaring fire.

"The snow might not let up for days," she reminded

him. "And while I'm glad we have a few animals on ice out there, it seems like you're begging for trouble, leaving them outside for so many animals to find them. Not to mention they're so far away from the house. I can't cook with them." She gestured to the three of them. "We need the food, not those wild animals. We have three hungry mouths to feed."

As if in a trance, Oscar shifted his gaze to the armchair where Rose slept. "I can fix that."

Her heart leapt to her throat. She shouldn't have said that. As she stood in shocked horror, Oscar reached for the gun in his holster. He always had it on him, didn't he? Always had a weapon at the ready and murder on his mind. He always accused her father of that, but Oscar spilled far more blood than her father ever did.

Mercy put a hand out toward him, trying to say something, anything, to get him to stop. But her mouth wouldn't move. It was like she was frozen from being able to say anything. It was like she was reliving that horrible dream all over again.

Instead of shooting, Oscar popped open the cylinder on his gun and narrowed his eyes. "I don't have a silver one for her though. Just regular ones in the chamber. That won't do. I'll have to fetch one from the shed." He closed up the cylinder and waggled an index finger into the air. "If I've got to go outside to get a silver bullet for Rose, I might as well check the traps too."

Running out of time. He will kill you.

Mercy glanced back at the fireplace and suddenly saw it with renewed perspective. How could she have been so oblivious? She had what she needed right here all along. She didn't need complicated plans, foolish plots. She just needed to open her eyes and look around her. Mercy knew in that moment what she had to do. She should have done it months ago, but she had been too scared, too afraid to do what needed to be done. She was so busy playing Oscar's game she had forgotten how to fight back.

While Oscar struggled to holster his gun back on his hip in his drunken haze, Mercy picked up the cast iron fireplace poker from beside the hearth. With shaking hands, she picked it up high over her head. She thought he would turn around and scream, but he didn't even look at her. He trusted her so completely he didn't suspect a thing.

Mercy brought the poker down on the back of Oscar's head. He screamed and stumbled forward. Blood seeped down the back of his neck, staining the collar of his shirt.

Dad had tried to keep her safe. He tried to keep her insulated from the world. But the world existed regardless of how many protections he put around her. Then Thomas tried to keep her protected, disguising her in plain sight. Wrappings and masks, vehicles and reputation, all of it was useless at the end of the day. There was no guaranteed safety.

Oscar tried to trap her here, keep her protected in his own twisted way, but that wasn't living. She wasn't going to be one of his pets like the werewolves outside. She had to break out of this trap if she ever hoped to be allowed to live. She was no squirrel or rabbit to be caught and killed at will.

There was no escape from this place unless Oscar died. Not later, not tonight, and not by someone else's hand. If Mercy wanted him dead, she would have to do it herself. She couldn't hesitate. She couldn't second-guess herself. She had to do it and get rid of the man who had tormented her for months. She had to get rid of the monster who had tried to turn her into his daughter.

Oscar stumbled forward and tripped over the dining table.

The scary part was it had almost worked there for a while. Mercy had started thinking of him as a father figure, calling him Pa without even realizing she had sometimes. She had started to fall into the safety and complacency he had taught her to have around him. She had fallen too hard into the role he wanted her to play and almost didn't crawl out of it. If her father hadn't come to her in that dream, if Rose's life hadn't been at risk, she might have lived as his daughter for the rest of her life.

"How dare you!" Oscar reached for the revolver on his hip and had it drawn in an instant.

Mercy brought the poker down again, this time on his shooting arm. He was trying to aim for her head, but the blow dropped the shot to the ground. She dove to the side as the bullet ricocheted off the cast-iron pot of soup still bubbling over the fire.

Rose screamed. The gunshot must have roused her from her daze. She scrambled slowly behind the armchair with bleary eyes. Even in a weakened state, she knew better than to stay in the open while Oscar had a loaded gun.

Oscar ducked, clearly fearing the bullet would come back for him. "Rose, get her! The girl has gone mad!"

Rose didn't leave the safe spot she had found, and Mercy took the opportunity to slam the fireplace poker into Oscar's foot. Blood seeped out of his shoe and created a small, growing puddle on the floor. Mercy remembered the stickiness of it from her dream. He screamed and fell backward. His head slammed hard into the heavy wood of the table.

He went still.

Mercy stared at Oscar, waiting for him to move, but he didn't. Was he dead? If not, how long would he stay down?

"Get the gun!" Rose hissed.

Mercy blinked and pulled the gun out of his hand. Blood pooled out of his shoe where Mercy had gotten his foot, spreading around his leg. There was some blood where his head had landed on the floor beside the table, but not as much as around his foot. He gave a rattled sound as he exhaled and Mercy jumped back.

"He's still alive!"

Rose got to her feet beside the chair, leaning heavily against it. "End this, Mercy. Shoot him!"

Mercy nodded. She dropped the fireplace poker onto the floor and held the gun out with both hands. It was the fastest and easiest way to end this, but the weapon shook in her hands. She had used a gun in Crowsmirth to kill a werewolf, but it was a sharp-toothed animal come to eat her and her friends. Oscar was human, someone who had known her parents. Her mother had known him well enough to ask him to keep an eye on Mercy and her dad. He was a kidnapper she had started to think of as a father, someone who claimed he just wanted to protect her. Could she dole out his death with the pull of a trigger?

She held up the gun and aimed it at Oscar's head. The handle was still warm from where he had gripped it, trying to kill her mere moments before. It would be so easy to pull the trigger, so why couldn't she do it?

"If you don't kill him, he will hunt you for as long as he lives. You know it! You've seen his anger, Mercy." Rose shook her head. "He wouldn't have hesitated a second to kill you if he wanted to. Why are you hesitating for him? He doesn't deserve your pity."

Mercy dropped her hands to her sides, shaking her head. "I've only had to shoot two people in my life, and both of them were transformed werewolves trying to eat me. I don't think I can do it to a person who is just unconscious. It feels… wrong."

Rose settled down in the armchair again, dragging up the blanket over herself. "Well, regardless, I don't think either of us has to worry about that monster any more. He just died. Look."

The hairs went up on the back of Mercy's neck. Sure enough, Oscar was no longer making his rattled breaths. His mouth hung partway open and the whites of his eyes were barely visible through his partly open eyelids. She stared at him for a full minute, but his chest didn't move. The fireplace poker had finished him. Slower, but just as effective as the gun.

"It's over," Mercy whispered. "It's finally over."

"He deserved far worse than a poker to the skull, but thank you for doing him in. I couldn't fight him any more even if I wanted to." Rose lowered her head and turned away from her. "I wanted to fight back. I honestly did."

"It got harder over time, didn't it?"

Rose nodded. "It shouldn't have. He was horrible! But I guess that's what happens when you live with a monster. Over time, you start to see them as human and you start to think they're not so different from you, even though they are." Rose leaned her head back against the cushion and closed her eyes. "I'm sorry I tried to get you to shoot him. That wasn't fair. I should have done it myself."

Mercy dropped the gun on the dining table. "It's okay, I couldn't do it either."

Rose gave a heavy sigh. "I am just so tired all the time these days. It's difficult."

Mercy gasped. "The cure," she cried. "Just stay put. And here's the gun, keep an eye on him just in case." She handed the gun over to Rose, careful not to step over Oscar's body. "I'll be right back!"

"Where are you going now?"

"To get you some help! If I can find the cure, that's the big question."

"Mercy, wait!" Rose called, but she didn't have time to wait. It was evening already, and nightfall would be coming soon. She needed to get Rose her cure before the transformation killed her.

Mercy ran out the front door. Finally, she was going to get inside the damn shed!

As soon as the door slammed behind her and she hurried down the porch steps did she realize what a bad mistake she had made.

10

HIDDEN SECRETS

THROUGH THE THICK **BLANKET** of falling snow, Mercy saw two pairs of golden eyes studying her. Jamison and Silver had both walked right up to the porch. They must have smelled the human blood inside and came closer to investigate, maybe even hoping to get a meal. Suddenly all the late night feedings and kind words were pushed aside in the face of fresh human food. At the end of the day they were still werewolves, even if they had been dosed with Liquid Lead. Some instincts even that compound couldn't remove.

Now that she was outside, she realized just how late it was. The gray clouds from the snowstorm all day had a way of confusing time. The cloudy sky made it dark early, so it was tough to know when nightfall was coming. The shorter days of winter made it even more difficult to figure out how much time was left. The transformation didn't wait for anyone, Oscar had been right about that at least.

Mercy had slim minutes left to get into the shed and

get a cure for Rose before she transformed. How many slim minutes? She had no idea. It could be ten, it could be fifty. Regardless, she needed that cure. That meant getting past these werewolves first.

With slow, careful footsteps, Mercy made her way out into the front yard. As her eyes adjusted to the light, she saw Silver had pulled his chain taut, drawing as close as he could to the porch. He would probably have been easier to get by on her way to the shed, but Jamison was actually closer to the shed than Silver.

Mercy could either take the long way around with Silver and have less trouble, or she could go the shorter path with Jamison. Always hungry Jamison, who got so excited over frozen squirrels he drooled icicles on his muzzle. It was probably a bad idea, but going with Jamison would be faster.

She glanced at the cloudy sky, wishing she could see how much daylight was left. She had no idea how much time she had, therefore she had no choice but to take Jamison's path. Even if it was more dangerous.

Careful, confident steps, that was the strategy. She headed off across the snow and toward the shed. Her stomach dropped at the clinking of a chain as Jamison panted closer and his big feet crunched down in the thick snow. He was behind her, panting so much, she could see his breath at her side. She could smell how rank it was too.

At first, Jamison was good. He just followed her a little too closely, clearly not good at respecting personal space. About halfway across his path, she was shoved forward and onto the ground. Her palms hit first, shoving snow forward as she braced herself. Cold snow spilled into her sleeves and down her shirt. She grunted in shock as she looked behind her at Jamison, trying to gauge what to do next.

Jamison wasn't snarling or even baring his teeth. But his nose was working overtime, sniffing at the air, and Mercy didn't like that.

"I don't have any food this time," she said, keeping her voice calm as she picked herself up off the ground. He circled around her, dragging his chain through the snow. His nose was all over her, working hard, and Mercy froze on instinct. Jamison might be the clumsier of the two werewolves, but he was a big wolf. On his back legs, he easily surpassed the height of the front door. She held her breath as he sniffed her hair, her face and, finally, her clothes. Did he think she was hiding a frozen squirrel in her jacket?

Wait… when she used the fireplace poker on Oscar, she saw blood on the back of his neck, but thought he hadn't bled much. Jamison clearly knew better, or at least his nose did. Some of Oscar's blood must have splashed onto her jacket. And it looked like Jamison was determined to get at it, even if he had to knock her to the ground to get her to stop. She didn't like being the target of his excitement, especially with his long claws and teeth.

Glancing up to the heavy snowfall and the clouds that were too dark, Mercy pulled off her jacket. The cold wind tore easily through her thin undershirt. Gooseflesh broke out over her body as she dropped the jacket to the ground and Jamison leapt on top of it. He tore through the cloth with ease and lapped at the front hungrily. Mercy didn't even see the blood he clearly enjoyed.

She would need to remember to bring some food for him later. Otherwise he might not let them leave.

With a calm pace and shivering from head to toe, Mercy headed for the shed. Finally, she stepped outside of Jamison's range and breathed a sigh of relief. At least she didn't have him all over her trying to get her clothes anymore. The wind picked up as she rounded around the corner of the house and her teeth started to chatter.

Before reaching the shed, she went to her bedroom window and slipped back inside. She pulled on a fresh sweater along with her trusty blanket. Her warm coat was lost, but at least she had a backup plan. Then she turned to her bed. She needed to grab one more item, just in case. She reached behind the headboard and grabbed the piece of splintered plate she had stowed away back there. It was a little dusty but just as sharp as the day she grabbed it.

Once upon a time, she imagined using it on Oscar. Instead, now it would have to do to help break into his shed.

Climbing back out into the snow, Mercy was no longer trembling. Good. She didn't want to survive Oscar only to die of hypothermia or lose a limb to frostbite. She was starting to feel proud of herself until she stood before the only place on the property she hadn't entered.

The shed was such a clumsy building, but it had eluded her for months. It taunted her through her bedroom window night after night. It nearly got her killed when she tried to force her way in the evening before. Now it stood without its protector and still it kept its secrets. Mercy was eager to see what was hidden inside.

"What were you hiding from me, Oscar?" she asked to the building. "What were you so frightened of Rose and I finding out?"

She started with the loose board she had found last night, working out the rusty nails using a corner of the blanket with frigid fingers. Oscar probably had the keys to this place on him, but she wasn't keen to check his body for them. There was no time for fiddling through his entire keyring, trying to find the right key for each of the half dozen padlocks he had on the door. That keyring had at least fifty keys. She would be there for hours trying to figure it out, and Rose needed the cure now.

Just as before, the long cold chains hung down in her face, freezing her nose and threatening frostbite to any patch of skin it stayed on for too long. Mercy resisted the urge to move them, but instead tried to avoid them lingering anywhere on her bare skin for long.

Finally the board came loose, revealing half a window. She pulled the wood down carefully with numb fingers. After a small bit of resistance she tugged the board down completely. Along with it came that horrible wailing whistle that rattled snow down on top of her head from the roof of the shed. Her ears hurt from the sound. She clamped her cold hands over her ears just as the sound finally died down.

Just before the whistle died, another sound had joined it, creating a horrible dissonance that made her wince. It was a human sound filled with anguish and pain, one she had heard every night for months, and she knew it well. In the silence that remained, Mercy looked back at the house in terror. She recognized the voice the scream belonged to.

Rose had transformed.

———

PUFFING clouds of panic into the air, Mercy scrambled into the shed through the half window. An oil lantern sat on a side table, along with matches. She had to bite her lips to keep her fingers still enough through the cold to use a match and light the wick.

A dim, tentative light filled the shed, shivering from the breeze that swept in through the open window and crept through the cracks in the walls. Mercy's mind ran a million miles a minute as she took in the space around her. Outside, the freezing wind howled and rattled the walls.

Oscar's ratty pickup truck sat in the middle of the shed, but not a single cobweb clung to its wheels. Of all the things he was a stickler for, apparently it was cleaning his own truck. He had been careful to take care of it, at least making sure it was in good enough condition to drive out of this place if he had to.

"Always ready to make an escape for yourself, Oscar. Why am I not surprised?" she whispered.

She pulled open the doors and searched the seats.

None of her belongings were there. Had he hidden them in his room all this time? Surely not. It would take hours to find the right keys for all the drawers in his bedroom and his closet too. Oscar probably had a whole stash of weaponry in there.

Her mind kept flicking to Rose, transforming right next to Oscar's body. At least she had fresh food to keep her occupied. But would it really distract her? Mercy thought of the way Rose stalked her at night and how she wasn't interested in frozen squirrels. She only seemed interested in murder. In particular, in Mercy.

"Damn it," she snapped. The cabin of the truck was empty. She checked all the compartments and hidden spots she could find. There wasn't even a set of keys to drive it. That was probably on him too. Along with all the other keys in this horrible place.

She turned to the walls of the shed. She had thought Oscar was a neat and tidy person based on how he kept the house, but over time, she realized that was Rose's doing against her will. The shed only Oscar could go into spoke a very different story. Years ago, Mercy had kept the shed so well organized she could grab what she needed in two minutes, max. Sure, it hadn't been the cleanest place, but it had been organized and she had prided herself on maintaining it. Now looking at the hobbled mess of dusty forgotten tools, she realized it would take her forever to find anything. The walls were covered in cobwebs and even a few spiderwebs. Her spare broom, the one she told him had been here in the shed, was exactly where she had left it, but it had been knocked to the ground.

Other than boarding up the windows, it looked like Oscar didn't do much to maintain this place. So why was he so worried about it when an intruder came on the grounds? Why had he gone inside to make sure nothing was missing, instead of checking the fence like she expected?

Mercy looked around and realized there were more than tools here. Boxes were everywhere. So many of them she couldn't count them all. They were piled up against the walls, lined up against each other, and shoved into corners. Was this it? Was this the secret Oscar was so protective of? She pulled a box out and held the lantern close as she looked inside. Small painting canvases. There had to be a dozen of them in this box alone. She picked one out of the box and saw the familiar eyes of her mother staring back at her, perfectly captured in paint.

Mercy gasped and dropped it back in. She pulled out another painting to see a forest. Another painting was a river. Another was the mill from years before. The paints were faded on many of them from time, some of them were even stuck together. Was Oscar really that protective of his paintings that he had to make sure they were safe? There had to be more than this here.

Wood slammed against wood. Mercy jumped, holding her lantern toward the window and looking at the house. The fire flickered in the wind. It was hard to see anything out there with how heavily the blizzard was coming down. Had a door slammed shut? Or maybe a table had been thrown across the room? She half expected to see Rose sprinting across the snow, red eyes gleaming.

"Okay, calm down. Time to think," she whispered to herself. "I'm Oscar. I've kidnapped a person and I don't know the value of what they had on them. Where do I hide their things?"

She pointed to the shelves. "Shelving? No, he keeps valuable paintings of my mom there and all his other, I guess, valuable paintings. He also has a few tools stowed here for a rainy day. Probably not there." She groaned and paced the limited floor space of the shed. "Oh, please don't tell me he threw them out! I don't know if I'll survive the night with Rose. And I can't kill her!"

Tears stung at her eyes. All she wanted was to escape this place and get back to her friends and loved ones. Oscar might be dead, but his death trap of a home may be the death of her yet.

A blistery wind swept in through the window and Mercy had to squint her eyes from it, making hot tears spill down her cheeks.

Something fluttered in the truck bed. She recognized the pattern of the quilt. Was that the blanket Jamison had when he was given the Liquid Lead in the front yard months ago? It was grimy and had a lot of bloodstains from his change, but that had to be it.

A few facts rapidly fired off in her mind: it was what Oscar would think would be a useless item, had belonged to someone he deemed to be disposable, and if left out in the open, it could potentially lead somebody back to the place if they found it. The bright colors of that blanket were definitely memorable.

She slid the oil lantern onto one of the workbenches and hauled herself up into the truck bed. She picked up Jamison's bloody blanket and shook off the dust and debris. But there was more than that. She found some clothes she didn't recognize with old, dark bloodstains. She recalled Oscar bragging about how many housekeepers he had before. This was what became of Oscar's pets when he was done with them. Their belongings were tossed into the back of his truck like trash. Probably taken somewhere and burned after he got too much to store here. She had no idea what happened to their bodies once they died. A burial if they were lucky. Burning bodies would be too noticeable. Maybe he just tossed them out to the werewolves to finish off. She winced.

Then she spotted it: her own satchel wadded up inside of some clothes she didn't recognize. Thankfully the satchel was closed, but that didn't fully protect the needles inside.

Several of the needles were broken, the chemical inside long ago evaporated. Looking at them all now, she wasn't even sure if they would work. No, they had to. Rose needed to be rescued from this curse. She had been through enough already.

Out of all the needles, only one seemed to be, maybe, viable. She dumped the discarded needles into the truck bed and pulled on her satchel. She cinched it around her waist and made sure the last needle was safe inside.

"I can make it work. I don't have a choice. I'm sorry,

Rose, this is the best we've got," she whispered to the open window.

Now all she needed to do was find Rose and administer the cure.

Mercy stared out at the dark, gray night, wondering how in the world she was going to do that.

MERCY DETERMINED she had two options to administer the cure to Rose. She could either go out into the blizzard and try to find her, possibly being stalked and killed in the process. Or she could wait it out in the shed, have a single, clear point of entry, and wait for her to come to Mercy. Considering how intent Rose had been on her previously, she thought waiting her out might be a better option.

So Mercy stared out through the open window and waited. The shed was a cramped space, and she only had one fragile oil lantern, but Oscar's piles of clutter would slow Rose down. Or at least she hoped it would.

After deciding against standing before the open window and allowing herself to be easily lunged at, Mercy chose a hiding place. The truck bed had an easy view out through the window and also allowed her the ability to duck down as needed. If this was going to work, she had to see Rose coming. If she let Rose ambush her, she wouldn't stand a chance to administer anything.

The blizzard only made things worse. Snow had already started piling up on the windowsill. She had maybe ten feet of visibility outside. Wind tore through the cracks in the shed and the oil lantern flickered helplessly against it. Mercy really didn't want it to go out. She appreciated having some light to see out here amid all the darkness.

Her knees dug into the freezing metal of the truck bed, and her legs kept cramping. At one point, she tossed the bloody clothes out the window, hoping it would lure in Rose, but the blood was so old she wasn't sure if it would do any good.

One leg throbbed with a cramp and Mercy shifted her weight with a groan. Where was she? It felt like she had been waiting in this shed for hours. There was no way to get comfortable and the longer she sat there staring out into the blizzard, the more her eyes played tricks on her. The more she thought she heard the clawing of nails on the shed. Sometimes the wind sounded like a werewolf's howl.

The memory of Rose's scream haunted her. It had mixed so well with the loud warning whistles Oscar had installed she was beginning to question what she heard. Instead of an enraged werewolf out to stalk her, maybe Rose was still inside. Maybe her transformation hadn't gone right, and she was in pain. Or in trouble.

What if Oscar had faked his death and fooled them both? She could easily see him doing that. Rose was certainly too weak to fight him off in her human form. Oscar was slippery enough for it.

Rose was right. Mercy should have shot him in the skull while she had the chance. At the very least she would know he wasn't hiding in wait for her back at the house. But she hadn't. Now Rose could be paying for her indecisiveness and her strange sense of honor. Since when did she care about honor when it came to killing people who wanted her dead? She blamed Oscar for putting that weird notion in her head, for making her hesitate when she should have simply shot him.

After waiting so long without seeing anyone coming, Mercy decided she had to go back to the house. She had to find out what had happened to Rose, and see for herself if Oscar was really dead. Sitting out in the blizzard waiting for answers would drive her mad otherwise. But she wasn't foolish enough to go back without some form of protection. She might have a cure for Rose in her hands, but she had to get close enough to administer it. Unless she could find her tools hidden away somewhere in this mess, an up close and personal administration was the only option, and she really didn't like that.

Oscar had one of her metal tubes when he had forced Mercy to change Jamison. Surely he had more of them lying around. She had used them for administering her darts of Liquid Lead, but it would be perfect for her needles too. Okay, maybe not perfect, but it would mean she didn't have to get in Rose's face to dose her. Despite the boxes she checked, the trash she sorted, or painted canvases she moved aside, she couldn't find a single one. Maybe that was another item that Oscar kept locked up in his room. Probably with the Liquid Lead.

With growing worry, she glanced to the open window and spotted something metal glinting in the candlelight. She shoved past a pile of boxes to reach it and pulled it down from its hook. It was a pair of prongs. She wound it up and an electric spark came to life between the spokes. They worked!

A werewolf howl in the distance tore away her joy. There was no mistaking it that time. It was not the wind. That sounded far away, maybe from the woods instead of from the house, but the blizzard could be morphing the sound. She held the prongs forward as she approached the window.

Swirling snow made it almost impossible to see the house, but that wouldn't have stopped Rose from hunting Mercy down if she was transformed. Mercy was the only human on the property. She wouldn't be able to help herself. Since she wasn't here, that meant something was wrong.

With her hands shaking, Mercy took a deep breath and climbed up into the window. She hopped down onto the powdery snow, keeping the prongs away from her body as she dropped.

Before she could fully regain her balance, something big and hairy lunged at her from the side of the shed. The eyes flashed red as though lit by an unearthly light from within, and Mercy realized her mistake. Rose wasn't hurt, she had been stalking her, waiting for Mercy to make a mistake. Like a fool, she had done just that. Rose had waited for her to grow impatient, to crawl out of the shed and make her presence known. Mercy had walked right into the trap.

Mercy sidestepped to avoid her, but her back hit the wall of the shed. Cold metal chains dug into her back. Out of sheer instinct, she shoved the prongs out at Rose, but Rose avoided the spokes with ease. As if she had done it a thousand times, she batted the prongs out of Mercy's hands with her front paws, touching the long handle and not the electrified prongs at the end. The prongs clattered onto the ground beneath the shed. When they touched the bare earth, they discharged. Mercy stared at Rose in horror.

Oscar must have tried to use the prongs on her before, maybe long before Mercy had shown up. But he must have tried to do it regularly, or at least often enough that the wolf in her recognized it and parried it away with ease. Mercy now understood her folly in thinking she could try to get close enough to administer the cure without one of the metal tubes. Rose was fast, agile, and knew she had the advantage with Mercy trapped out in the blizzard with her. Mercy was merely a slow, sluggish human pretending to be a hunter.

Rose stalked closer, baring sharp canines and her long claws. Her eyes shined a bright red gleaming brighter through the swirling snow. She took her time. She acted like she had waited a long time for this. Mercy shook her head, wishing she had something, anything, to use as a weapon.

After everything she had survived, was this really how it would end? Torn to shreds at her childhood home by a werewolf she was trying to save?

"Not here," Mercy whispered, begged. "Please, not like this."

Her words only seemed to enrage Rose. Mercy flinched as clawed talons ripped across her right cheek. Mercy screamed. She fell to the frozen ground. Cold metal pressed into her back. She looked up into the gray sky and felt her tears mixing with blood on her face.

Rose leaned her head back and howled into the sky. Victory. In the distance, many voices answered. A primal fear took hold of Mercy and she looked for the prongs, but they had been shuffled too far beneath the shed for her to reach them.

Red eyes locked with hers, and Mercy knew what was next. She had seen it several times before, hadn't she? The sheriff in Kanta, the grocer at Crowsmirth, and all the bodies from that long, horrible night she had spent there. They went for the stomach first, sometimes the neck. At least from the attacks she had seen, that's what they preferred.

A cold wind tore between them, freezing Mercy's tears as blood dripped down her neck. Chains drummed against the shed like a warning.

Mercy blinked. The chains!

With a cry, she reached around her and grabbed as many of the chains as she could hold in two hands. Then she tugged as hard as she could.

The whistles screamed in a disjointed chorus, louder than the wind, louder than the werewolf howls. Mercy winced at the sound, but Rose leaped back as if struck. She turned her head to one side then the other, clearly panicking. She scrambled in the snow in confusion before loping away across the yard.

Mercy released the chains and let the noise dissipate.

She did it. She scared her off.

With a groan, she crawled up to her feet and picked up her blanket that had fallen into the snow. This time, she wouldn't take any chances. This time she wouldn't forget her training all those years ago.

Shaking from head to toe, she crawled back inside the shed. Nails and a hammer, that's what she needed. She dragged several chains inside before nailing up the gaping window. It wasn't perfect, but it didn't need to be to keep a werewolf out. It just needed to hold for the night.

When she was done, Mercy dragged herself into the truck bed and pulled the chains toward her. She hooked them on the edge, now and then tugging on them to let their warnings tear through the night. It was loud enough to compete with the storm and loud enough to frighten off a werewolf.

Mercy blew out the oil lantern and refilled it before lighting it again. She turned up the flame, letting the warm light reveal every wall of the shed. It was going to be a long night.

She held the blanket to her face to stop the bleeding and listened as the wind howled.

There would be no sleep tonight.

11

LINGERING GHOSTS

THE NIGHT SEEMED TO LAST forever. At one point, Mercy accidentally nodded off and had to do a check on the entire shed and lay on the chains for several minutes before she felt safe. She lay with the oil lantern curled up with her bloody blanket, listening for any sounds that Rose had returned.

After being afraid of dozing off a second time, Mercy spent a large part of the night sawing off the hinges on the shed door. Those many locks had been made to keep out people not werewolves, and Mercy wanted an easier escape route if she needed it.

When dawn eventually broke, Mercy pulled open the shed door and stepped out into the early morning light. She was met with a gray dawn. She had seen no more signs of Rose during the night, and she was glad of it.

The snow had finally stopped falling, but the clouds hadn't departed. They hung heavy over the sky like a giant blanket. From her estimate, it looked like at least two feet of snow had fallen overnight.

Mercy yawned and stretched her weary arms. Every muscle in her body yearned for sleep, but that would have to wait. She wasn't the only one who had a rough night. And she had a cure to administer.

Walking around to the front yard, she saw Jamison had turned her jacket into a nest and was fast asleep with it underneath him. Silver was bundled up as close to the house as he could get, using a portion of the roof as an overhang. He drowsily watched her with amber eyes.

"Any idea where Rose is, Silver?"

He simply stared at her. It looked like he hadn't gotten much sleep last night either. With Rose running around loose, she wasn't surprised by that.

Hopefully the dried blood on her cheek didn't give him any ideas. She didn't want a repeat with Jamison and the jacket. She would have to wash her face inside to be safe.

She walked the full perimeter of the house, no longer scuttling near the fence line or wary of Oscar's constant presence. Freedom smelled crisp. She let the air fill her lungs and breathed it out, feeling alive like she hadn't felt in months.

No signs of Rose. She couldn't have gotten out of the fence, could she? She went by the power house and made sure the windmill was still turning. Everything outside looked to be in order.

That left indoors.

The back door was locked from the inside, so with a

huff, Mercy climbed in through her bedroom window. She was so tired she almost fell on her face, but then she got her balance again. She pulled the blanket down from the window, no longer needing to hide her actions, no longer needing to sneak around her own home. She went to her water basin and washed her face with icy water, crying out as it touched her face. She would need to put more on the wounds besides water later, but it would wait.

Rose wasn't in her room and she wasn't in the hall-way. She looked toward the living room, but that would be the last place she searched. After being awake all night, she didn't have the stomach to check the living room yet. Not when Oscar's body was prob-ably a mutilated mess out there. So she checked Oscar's bedroom.

Puddles of blood scattered the room. They were on the floor, the bed quilt, and even splashed up on the walls. Curled up in the bed beneath the covers was Rose, sleeping as soundly as if she hadn't almost eaten Mercy alive overnight. It was a morbid sight, but one she had grown accustomed to being around werewolves all the time.

Mercy hated to wake her, knowing that she needed to sleep to recover, but she wanted to get the cure into her as soon as possible.

"Rose?" Mercy nudged her shoulder. "Wake up, it's just me."

Her eyelids fluttered with a heaviness Mercy felt all too well.

"Mercy?" Her eyes opened fully, then her mouth

dropped open. "Oh my gosh, your face! Did I do that to you?"

She nodded. "It's not as bad as it probably looks. Don't worry about it. You aren't the first werewolf I've been fortunate enough to survive." She reached into her satchel and pulled out the dose of her cure, the only one left from the batch she had originally taken to Crowsmirth. "I need to give you this."

"What is it?" Her brow furrowed.

Mercy hadn't even gotten the chance to explain the full details, had she? Everything had happened so quick and with Oscar around there was never time to do anything. "It's a cure, sort of. You'll be able to change at will instead of every full moon. But it does have drawbacks."

Rose put out her arm, but Mercy held up a hand.

"Wait, just listen to me. It's experimental still! It could work, but it could also kill you. This dose has been sitting in Oscar's truck for months, so I honestly have no idea if it would even work on you. It could do nothing, or it could hurt you. I don't know."

"Just give it to me," Rose demanded with tired eyes. "This… beast inside of me is going to kill me soon. I can feel it clawing its way out of me, feeding on me from the inside out. I don't want to die that way, Mercy. If you have an alternative, even if it kills me, I'd rather take every chance I can get. I nearly killed you last night. You can act like that scratch isn't much, but if I was close enough to do that, I was close enough to do worse."

Mercy sighed. "I mean, you're right. It wasn't pretty.

And I'm probably a wreck right now." She held up the needle. "Are you sure about this? There's no taking it back."

Rose closed her eyes. "Yes, I'm sure. Just get it over with. I really don't like needles."

Mercy obliged. After last night, she wasn't going to argue.

—————————

IT WAS afternoon by the time Mercy awoke from a deep, dreamless sleep. She smelled pancakes and smiled. The cure must have helped Rose feel a lot better. Mercy couldn't remember the last time Rose felt well enough to try to cook.

Her body protested as she rolled out of bed. She had once again slept fully clothed, but she didn't care. She yawned, but stopped quickly at the pain in her right cheek.

She had forgotten about that. She touched the cuts, only to feel taped bandages instead. Her eyes went wide.

"Rose?" she called into the kitchen. "Did you bandage me up?"

Laughter was her response. "Good afternoon to you too! And you're welcome. You needed something on those!"

Mercy shook her head and headed out for breakfast. "You seem to be feeling better."

Rose laid out a plate of pancakes. "I feel like I've been given a second chance at life, Mercy. I really do."

She swept over, smiling and beaming despite the bags under her eyes. "You saved my life. Thank you."

"No, you were hurt because of me. You didn't deserve that." Mercy yawned. "You deserved to live without Oscar ordering you around all the time."

She frowned as she turned over a pancake. "That man was a monster."

"Hey, I thought you said you couldn't bake. Don't pancakes count as baking?"

Rose laughed, "No, I said I burned everything I baked. Don't worry, I left a burned one at the bottom of your stack. I was hoping you wouldn't notice, but since you had to go and call me out on it."

Mercy pursed her lips to keep from laughing. Smiling hurt right now. She dug into her plate of pancakes, but she couldn't help but glance over to where Oscar's body had fallen. Rose had moved the dining table and chairs aside and a rug was in the space his body had lay, but the dark bloodstain could still be seen underneath it.

"Don't worry about him. I took care of it." Rose sat down opposite her with her own pile of pancakes. Many of hers were more burned than Mercy's.

"Do I want to know how?"

"Well," she said, cutting into a steaming one on top. "Let's just say that I was surprised at my strength when I went to take him out back. You didn't mention that with your cure."

Mercy laughed and winced at the pain. "Yeah, I didn't want to get your hopes up. Like I said, I wasn't sure if it would even work on you."

"It worked great. And Oscar is very much gone." Rose paused a moment before diving into her pancakes again.

"Thank you," Mercy said. "I don't think I could have done it."

"I know. You couldn't even pull the trigger. I wasn't going to make you touch his corpse. Don't worry. After what you did for me, that was nothing."

Mercy smiled and winced again. As glad as she was to be finally rid of Oscar, she wouldn't feel fully comfortable until they left. She was tired of the ghosts that lingered here.

———

IT WAS mid-afternoon when they finally had the truck idling at the front gate of the property. Mercy had found the keys inside Oscar's nightstand. Oscar's beat up truck was even older than her father's had been. The headlights flickered hesitantly, but she only had to crank it once to get it to start. She only needed it to last until they got to Farrell Mill. Then it could fall apart all it wanted.

Some of the snow had started melting, but it would still be a difficult road to Kanta. They would have to drive slower to get through the snow and avoid fallen branches, but Mercy knew they could make it. Once they made it to the main road, it should be easier.

"Is it a good idea to leave this late?" Rose asked.

"Trust me when I say we do not want to enter Kanta during the day. This way, we'll arrive right at dusk, when most people are already closed up for the night. We head to the mill and they'll let us in quick."

Rose shook her head. "I don't know if I like this plan, but you know this area better than I do."

Mercy opened the door to climb into the driver's seat. She looked back at the house, at the shed, and at the power house in the distance. Something was missing. She had that nagging feeling like she was forgetting something all day and she couldn't figure out what it was. Just as she was about to hop in, she realized what it was: the only thing she wanted to preserve from this place. "Hang on, I'll be right back!"

"Where are you going now?"

"Forgot something!" She trotted back to the front of the house, stepping cautiously around the thick snow. Neither Jamison nor Silver gave her any mind. She had given them each a pile of frozen animals after emptying all the traps. They had a dozen each that ought to keep them satisfied for a few days.

Through the front door and into the living room she ran, dropping snow and ice off her boots as she went. Finally she came to a stop before her mother's portrait. She stared up at her mother's perfect portrait, at her smile that held mirth and secrets.

"I hate that you let Oscar make this beautiful painting of you, Mom. I really have no idea if it's accurate or not. But Dad loved it and I always have too. It's all I have of you. I can't just leave you here anymore. I know Farrell Mill isn't exactly a pretty place, but I think you'll look great there."

The portrait stared back at her with colors perfectly

captured, forever frozen in time. Mercy pulled over one of the dining chairs and climbed up on it to pull the painting down. It was heavier and more awkward than she expected, but she didn't drop it.

She pulled her blanket off of her bed and wrapped it around the canvas. It wasn't much, but it ought to hold until they got to Kanta.

Rose was grinning as Mercy awkwardly carried it down the porch and across the front yard. She started laughing when Mercy tried to wedge the painting between them.

"Hang on, let me just carry it, crazy woman. It'll get torn up on this snowy road otherwise."

"I had to get it! It didn't feel right leaving her here." Mercy went around to open the latch of the electrified gate before using the kick to open it with her foot. Then she hopped in and drove through. She got out once more to get the gate closed behind them, but Rose put a hand on her arm.

"Wait, what about those two?" She nodded in the direction of Silver and Jamison. "They'll be locked in by themselves with no food."

"I'll come back out with Thomas in a few days and we'll bring them back to the mill. They can't be cured because of the Liquid Lead Oscar gave them. Remember what I told you?"

"Yes, but…" She glanced back to them again and spoke in a soft voice. "It just feels unfair is all. They're prisoners still and we aren't."

"Don't worry, we'll come back for them. I promise." She hopped out of the truck and closed the gate. She waved to Silver, who gave a big yawn and huddled down to go back to sleep. Jamison nestled down into her jacket with his back turned toward her. Clearly, they were just fine with them leaving.

Mercy hopped back in the truck, ready to take the road back to Kanta and back to her real home.

THE ROAD back to Kanta was not as easy as she had hoped. Mercy expected branches down here and there, but not entire trees. She had put some tools into the bed of the truck, an ax and one of Oscar's whistles from his shed, but she hadn't really expected to need them.

"What are we going to do?" Rose asked as they stared at the fallen tree in front of them.

Mercy sighed. "Get the ax, I guess."

"Do we have time for that?"

"No, but do we have a choice?"

Mercy hopped out to get the ax, and Rose joined her, setting the painting carefully into her seat. "No offense, but it's going to take hours to cut through that with an ax. We don't have hours."

Mercy picked up the ax out of the truck bed. "Do you have a better idea?"

Rose thought for a moment and turned to the fallen pine that blocked their path. "Actually, I do. You said I can change at will, right?"

Mercy hopped down from the truck. "Yeah, but I don't recommend changing your whole body, not yet anyway. You haven't had enough time to recover from—"

With some effort, Rose shifted her arm into a werewolf arm. "That wasn't as hard as you made it out to be!"

Mercy laughed and rubbed at her bandaged cheek. "I mean, I've not done it before!"

Rose raked her claws over the pine, once, twice, three times, and the tree was cut in two.

Gaping at the progress, Mercy tossed the ax back into the truck bed as Rose picked up half the tree with a grunt and tossed it off the road. Then she picked up the other half and tossed it aside too.

"You—you didn't have to get both. I could have made it by on half the road," Mercy urged.

Rose was grinning ear to ear. "This was fun! I hope we run into more trees!" She shifted her arm back, flinging blood off of her arm and onto the snow.

They were off again and only hit one more fallen tree before they finally made it to the main road. Even though Rose was making short work of the pine trees, Mercy really missed the Tortoise Thomas built for them. At one point the truck almost got stuck in a snowdrift and Rose had to push while Mercy floored it. Finally the sad, whiny vehicle made it out. She was afraid to push it hard again after that. She wasn't sure if it would make it. The headlights barely gave off any light and she wasn't sure how much more it could take.

When the trees broke and Kanta finally came into view, tears streamed down Mercy's cheeks. She never in her life thought she would cry to see that ugly city again, but here she was. She had missed it so much in all its worn-out glory. It wasn't quite dusk. Rose moving trees from the road had made it a lot faster to get here, but the roads were still deserted. A little earlier than normal, but considering the bloodbaths happening at Crowsmirth, she wasn't that surprised.

As the truck puttered along the dirt road and Mercy got closer to Farrell Mill, she felt her heart leap into her throat.

In all the time Mercy had lived and worked at the Mill, its constant plume of steam into the sky had become a balm of consistency in her chaotic life. As she pulled up to the enormous gates and looked upwards, not a single plume of steam was visible in the dwindling light. She couldn't even hear any of the grinders moving.

Something terrible had happened in her absence and Mercy feared what they might find beyond the gate.

To be completed in
Book 5: The Howl of Kanta

Despite The Fury of Kanta being such a tough book to write, it was also one of my favorites. I really enjoy writing villains who have sparks of kindness, or heroes that who have shades of darkness. I enjoy exploring morally gray characters. It's why I loved playing with the dynamic between Oscar and Mercy. It was fun to revisit Mercy's family home and flesh out her family history that she missed out on. I also enjoyed crafting Oscar's downfall over the years that led him here.

This book felt like I was sitting down right beside Mercy the entire time and transcribing her story. It was an oddly personal experience and a real joy to explore. I thought of it almost like a character story for her and Oscar, and it was interesting to see what happened as the snow piled up outside and their frazzled nerves began to break.

I hope you enjoyed this book as much as I did writing it. It's certainly the most unsettling book in this series so far.

I look forward to having you back for The Howl of Kanta, the fifth and final book in The Wolves of Kanta series!

Standalone

Short stories, horror, dark fantasy

The Impostor and Other Dark Tales

Weird western, werewolves, vampires, short story

Night Feeders

Mystery, film noir, humor, short story

The Mysterious Disappearance of Charlene Kerringer

 **Join the Mailing List** 

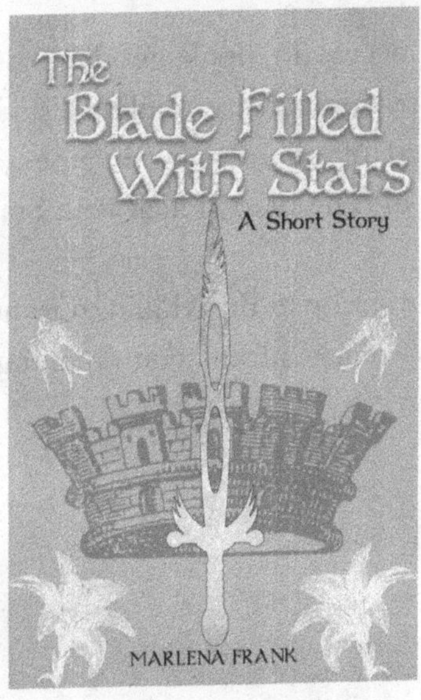

The Blade Filled with Stars

A kingdom is under siege from a familiar enemy. Families and friends are pitted against each other without reason. Slaughter is imminent while the winged Queen Khafil soars overhead. Desperate and terrified, Anna works with her sister, Lilah, to summon aid from their mother's ancient spell book.

Determined to save their people, the sisters

summon Death to help them, but Death is not easily swayed. Neither of the sisters are prepared for the consequences.

Want a peek behind the scenes?
Want to preview my books before they get released?

Get exclusive access to book goodies, giveaways, and cover reveals by joining my mailing list. Not only will you get notified of all my new releases, you'll get an exclusive copy of The Blade Filled with Stars.

Subscribe to the Mailing List at:
http://marlenafrank.com/mailinglist/

Follow me on Ko-Fi for regular updates on my writing progress.

Monthly subscribers get access to sneak peeks at stories way before anyone else. They also get access to cover reveals, monthly shout-outs on social media, and thanked by name in the acknowledgements in my books.

http://ko-fi.com/MarlenaFrank

ACKNOWLEDGMENTS

The Fury of Kanta could never have been written without the help of many. Writing a book is a collaborative effort. There are many people I want to thank for their help with making The Fury of Kanta come to life.

Lara Zielinsky is the editor who has been with this series since The Blood of Kanta and has helped to not only fix the grammar issues, but has also shaped this story into its best form. She has been incredibly helpful on each of the books she's worked on with me and I look forward to hearing her feedback on each book because she helps so much!

Harvest Moon Designs did an incredible job with designing the covers for this entire series, and The Fury of Kanta has perhaps my favorite of the bunch. I love the framing of the trees and the branches, and I love the posing and the crows in the background. I'm grateful to them for not only honing in on the style for this series, but really digging into it.

Once again, I have to thank my older sister, Kelley, who is a constant support with my books. Even when we had a bunch of events to attend, she encouraged me to keep going with my series. She's kept me going when I wasn't sure if I would get everything done in time. I'm endlessly grateful to her for her help and her support.

To my parents for always supporting my author career in any way they can. They are willing to help me whenever I need it, listen to my indie publishing woes, and have been at my side through it all. They applaud me with every milestone. I'm so lucky to have parents who support my writing career.

To my aunt Charmaine for cheering me on with every piece I write. She is always following my work and has read just about everything I've ever written. She always has a kind word, a wise thought, and gives encouragement regardless of what I'm struggling with.

Thank you to Candace Robinson and Carla Lewis, two women who have inspired and supported me through so much on this terrifying indie publishing path. You both are always there for me and are such amazing writers. I'm always in awe of the work you both produce. I feel so privileged to have you as friends and to have your support.

A big thank you to Donna who has been one of my longest readers and Ko-Fi monthly supporters. She has not only given me some wonderful inspiration for some upcoming projects, but she has been a constant supporter of all the crazy ideas I talk about on my Ko-Fi page. Over the years, she's become a friend whose opinion I trust and appreciate. I am incredibly grateful to have her as one of my constant readers and supporters.

Thank you, dear reader, for being here. The Fury of Kanta wouldn't exist without your support. In fact, The Wolves of Kanta series as a whole would never have

gotten far without you. Thank you for being here and I
hope to see you in the last book in this series: The Howl
of Kanta!

ABOUT THE AUTHOR

Marlena Frank is the author of young adult fantasy and horror novels, short stories, novellas, and book series. Many of her books have hit the bestseller charts, including her debut novel, Stolen. Her work has been praised by Readers' Favorite and featured in De Mode of Literature Magazine. Her stories have appeared in anthologies such as Emporium of Superstition, Catstruck!, Heroic Fantasy Quarterly, Georgia Gothic, and The Sirens Call ezine.

Although born in Tennessee, Marlena has spent most of her life in Georgia. She lives with her sister and two spoiled adopted cats. She serves as the Vice President of the Atlanta Chapter of the Horror Writers Association, is an active member of the Science Fiction and Fantasy Writers Association, and is an avid member of the Atlanta cosplay community.

She is also an INFJ, a tea drinker, and a wildlife enthusiast.

Support her on Ko-Fi: ko-fi.com/MarlenaFrank
Follow her at: MarlenaFrank.com